THE
BUTTERFLY
SHELL

MAUREEN WHITE was born in Canada where she was one of the founders of Toronto's Nightwood Theatre. In Ireland she has worked as a writer, director, teacher and dramaturg. Maureen has co-written the plays *This Is For You Anna* (published by Playwrights Canada) and *Unravelling the Ribbon* (with Mary Kelly, published by Nick Hern Books). As dramaturg for Rough Magic Theatre Company, Maureen works on the development of new plays. She is also the First Year Acting Teacher at the Gaiety School of Acting. *The Butterfly Shell* is her first novel.

MAUREEN WHITE

These are a couple of things I always wear my butterfly shell — No.2 I don't cut myself anymore. I know sounds weird — this year I took a year but more white sheet over your head in a way maybe spirits do exist kind of way. The doctors think it's all part of post traumatic stress — that after an accident

I don't cut myself anymore that you don't know. No.3 I don't even when I'm sunny or clammy No.3 I believe in ghosts — always it's in a wanna not good as in a do-it-yourself had anyone had anyone bread way sun is freshly down on me white teeth that

THE
BUTTERFLY
SHELL

THE O'BRIEN PRESS
DUBLIN

First published 2015 by The O'Brien Press Ltd
12 Terenure Road East, Rathgar, Dublin 6, Ireland
Tel: +353 1 4923333
Fax: +353 1 4922777
books@obrien.ie
www.obrien.ie

ISBN: 978-1-84717-678-3

10 9 8 7 6 5 4 3 2 1
20 19 18 17 16 15

Printed and bound by CPI Group (UK) Ltd, Croydon, CR0 4YY
The paper in this book is produced using pulp from managed forests.

The O'Brien Press receives assistance from

For

Luke and Aoife

and in memory of

Paul Joseph Conlon and Gerard O Callaghan

and all the little souls who left too early

First.

There are a few things about me you should know.

1. I always wear my butterfly shell – even when I'm
    swimming or sleeping.
2. I don't cut myself any more.
    and
3. I believe in ghosts.

Which I know sounds weirder than numbers 1 and 2 but
if you had the kind of year I had maybe you would believe too. Not ghosts as in a white sheet over your head
at Halloween kind of way but more in a maybe spirits do
exist kind of way.

The doctors told Mam I might have some 'post-
traumatic stress', that after an accident it's quite normal

to feel disoriented. I don't feel disoriented. The sun is beating down on me while I write this and it's been hot and sunny every day since I arrived. I read in the paper this is the warmest and driest summer on record in Connemara since 1995. I'm looking out at the sea and everything seems crystal clear.

I'm glad now I kept a diary. I might have to use it sometimes to be sure I'm being accurate, but mostly I remember everything that happened this year. Lots of weird things happened even before the accident. So I guess I'd better start at the beginning.

The beginning of First Year.

Here goes.

1

I was a bit nervous the day before my first day of secondary school. Just the normal amount of nervous I think. I had my uniform ready and a new pencil case and bag. I wished I knew more girls going to the school but really I was fine. In primary school there were twelve girls and thirteen boys in my class. Four of the girls were going to the Tech (which is mixed), five to the posh private school on the Green and Deborah Walshe and Bea Carpenter who were already best friends and always glued together and never talked to anyone else and me – we were the only ones going to St Bridget's School in Rathmines.

Dad said it was ridiculous to go anywhere but local and he didn't think for one second that private schools were any better than the regular ones. 'And as for the tuition? Are they mad?' So I had a feeling that even if we were rich (which we aren't by the way – just average as far as I can tell) I wouldn't be going to the Green which suited me fine as I'd rather walk to school.

Mam and Dad hardly ever go out at the same time and in fact my mam rarely – and I mean rarely – leaves the house at all these days so when they did go out and said they'd be back in a half hour, I thought I'd take advantage of their exit.

It really was a spur of the moment thing that made me go into Mam and Dad's bedroom to borrow some of Mam's perfume. My mam loves perfume. She has a different smell for each mood and I love her lavender one. She hadn't worn it for ages. My plan was to take it to school with me and put it on just before I got there and then wash it off before coming home.

I don't know what I was thinking. It isn't as if borrowing perfume is something that is easy to get away with. My mam always notices even if there is the slightest smell of something and she always knows exactly what it is. She can smell when I've made hot chocolate – hot chocolate! – which doesn't even have a smell as far as I can tell.

The small pale blue bottle of perfume called Linen Sky that Mam got for her birthday was on top of her dresser but not the lavender one. That's the one I wanted because it reminded me of Mam from when I was little, when we would go away for summer holidays. Once we even went to Canada to visit Aunt Kate. Mam wasn't so big then and she smelled like lavender all the time. I guess I kind of wanted to hold onto a summer feeling and even though I had no intention of snooping, I opened the top left-hand small drawer to see if it was there. And that's when I saw the box.

It was a beautiful wooden box with the lid held on with an elastic band and before I knew what I was doing I had it in my lap and was opening it. It was full of letters on cream paper. I took them out and promised myself I would only look at the top one. It was folded in half so I opened it. It was in Mam's handwriting.

Dear Marie who would be one today,
I wish you were here – to start to walk
– to call me Mama – to smile and already
have favourite things.
I love you.

The next letter was also to Marie but before I got a chance to read it I heard a sound at the front door. I sort of froze – just literally stood there holding onto the box instead of putting it away and legging it out of there. They must have forgotten something and that's why they came back so soon. My heart was beating so hard I was sure they could hear it and then I could feel my neck and face getting hot and red which I hate and which happens sometimes when I don't know what to do. I didn't hear anything more – maybe it was just someone putting a flyer through the letter slot. I really would make a terrible professional thief because by then my hands felt all sweaty and I didn't want to get the letters wet so I shoved them back in the box and back into the drawer and ran out of the room.

It didn't matter that I only had time to read one. I got the picture: they were love letters to the perfect child. Letters about how much she was missed, this child who had the same name as me.

I never did find the perfume.

I went to my room and read until dinner.

*

It didn't take long to walk to St Bridget's. At the end of our street is Leinster Road. Straight down that for seven minutes and then right onto Clareville Avenue and at the end of it are the trees. That was something I liked about this school even before I knew I was going there – it's surrounded by trees and doesn't feel like it's in the middle of the city which it nearly is. By the gate there is a willow tree that kind of sweeps over the sign with the name of the school on it. I hope they never cut it back although I wouldn't be surprised if they did because now all you can see is 'get's Secondary School'.

Just as I was getting to the school I saw a girl come out of her house, cross the street and go straight to the willow tree. Imagine living right across the street from the school. How lucky is that? If you went to bed with your uniform on you could sleep in until you heard the first bell and still be on time. When I got closer I could see she was busy writing something on the ground with her foot. I could tell she was weird from a mile off. But I could also kind of tell that she didn't care. She looked at me looking at her and said, 'Hi I'm Stella Stella.' She sort of whispered the second Stella which I thought was an unusual way to introduce yourself. Later that day in school whenever the teacher said anything she did the same weird repeating thing. Like when the teacher said, 'Open your books to page 15, Class', right away Stella whispered really quietly to herself 'to page 15, Class.'

I said, 'I'm Marie.'

She said, 'Hi Marie Marie,' and looked back at her feet so I just went into the school.

There was actually another Marie in my class. Her hair was dead straight and she was Polish, and on that first day, Rachel Quinn (who you could tell a mile off was not weird and was probably the opposite of Stella) decided that Marie was gorgeous and should be her friend and so she was Marie and then Rachel started calling me Other Marie. I couldn't believe it when she said that – not that I minded having a nickname, it's just that one.

Rachel must have seen my reaction because she wouldn't stop using it.

And in no time she had our home teacher, Miss Featherston, under her spell. When she was switching our seats after lunch Miss Featherston actually called me Other Marie.

Rachel Quinn is beautiful by the way and knows it. She already had loads of friends because they all went to St Mary's Primary School together. And I bet she'd have had loads of friends even if she didn't already know them. She's that kind of person. The uniform looked so good on her and her perfect blonde hair made me sick. I would have loved to sit behind her in class and just cut a huge chunk out. Can you imagine her face when she noticed?

Mam says I am lucky to have naturally curly hair and that people pay to have their hair look like mine. That I cannot imagine even though on my last report card from primary school it said, 'outstanding imagination and command of the English language'.

I never know how to wear my hair it's so frizzy. I'm not sure if it looks better tied back in a ponytail or just out with a hairband. Mam says I should just stop fighting it and before I know it curly hair will be all the rage. I don't think so but then my mother was never going to be a good one to know what is 'all the rage'. But I do like that expression – even if she is the only one I've ever heard use it. Rage is right.

*

Day two was when it started.

I tried to smile when Rachel called me Other Marie but I could tell she didn't really like me. I felt like she was testing me. It was like her eyes looked through me and she had already decided that I wasn't interesting but that I might be interesting to torment.

It didn't take long to find out what the day held in store for me and it was kind of my fault. I thought that in the morning everyone was leaving their bags down at the windowsill at the end of the first floor hall. Turns out it was just Rachel and a girl who might have been Claire and Jill who had put their bags there and when I went to get mine they were laughing at it. 'It's so ugly it looks like it was bought in the Heron Gate Warehouse,' Rachel said.

Now I suppose I should have said something at that point but I was sort of paralysed and I just stood there waiting for them to put it down. The thing is they were right. It *was* from the Warehouse and I hadn't really cared till that moment. I did have my eye on a turquoise bag in town but when Mam said, 'Don't be ridiculous we aren't paying that much for a bag' in her voice that meant 'this is not up for discussion' I hadn't said another word. Had I only known what would happen I might have made a case for the turquoise bag, voice or no voice.

When Rachel said, 'Let's see whose it is,' I knew I had to say it was mine. But something seemed wrong with my throat and when I walked up to take it, nothing came out. 'Other Marie, is this yours?' Rachel asked in a really fake voice. 'We had no idea. Let's see what you have in it. I mean we're all going to show what we have so you may as well too.'

For a second I thought that meant she wanted me to hang out with them but then I saw her looking at Claire and Jill and you could tell they wanted to laugh and I wanted to run away from them as fast as I could.

Rachel went first. She had a cosmetic case with make-up – actual make-up as in real foundation not just tinted moisturiser, lip gloss, mascara, three pens from the Pen Place shop and a gorgeous little key ring with a silver cat on it for her locker key. Her lunch was in a flowery plastic box that looked more like a jewellery box than a lunch box. And she had pink tissues and a silver binder with loads of poly pockets.

'Here you go Other Marie,' said Rachel and she held out my bag for me. But somehow she managed to turn it upside down when she was handing it to me and everything fell out – and I mean everything – my navy blue binder, my babyish pencil case with a rainbow on it –

no make-up bag – and an ordinary key ring with some yellow tape on it so I could keep my home key separate from my locker key. Rachel 'helped' me pick everything up saying each item in her really fake nice voice that I knew she used to make the others laugh. 'Here Other Marie, don't forget your rainbow pencil case.'

I felt my neck and face get hot and when I looked at her I knew it had started. Rachel had decided that I would be the one she would get and I knew I wasn't imagining it but I didn't really understand it. I don't think it was just that my things weren't cool. I think she saw something in my eyes when she first called me Other Marie and I know that isn't something that would stand up in a court of law but I do know it started then.

I kept reminding myself that I would soon be home and then I could read more of my book. The rest of the day passed pretty quickly.

Our last class was English and we got to work right away. The teacher, Mr McGuire, seemed amazing even though he was almost completely bald. He read the first chapter of *The Boy in the Striped Pyjamas* out loud and told us our homework was to describe the characters from Chapter 1. Lots of people started complaining that we shouldn't have homework because it was only day two but I had a feeling that it was because they weren't really listening when he was reading and so they didn't have a clue what to do.

I decided to do my homework as soon as I got home. It was very easy and hardly took any time at all so when I finished I kept on writing and in my extra A4 pad I described all the girls in the class. I'm going to call this my File Pad. I'm not sure what I'll do with it but Dad always says 'trust your gut' and my gut told me to keep track of who was who. Plus it was good practice for when I become a writer.

I was reading an absolutely fabulous book, a really old one my cousin sent me from Canada. It was called *Janis of City View* and was about a girl who got leukaemia but she never ever complained and was really nice to the little kids in the hospital and then she died but first she donated her eyes so some blind person could have them.

I always wonder if that means you will see the world the way your donor did. And maybe you would have some of their memories. I wonder if that's possible. I read a short story in a magazine when I was waiting for my dad at the dentist's and it was about a girl who had a heart transplant and then she fell in love at first sight when she was on a plane and it turned out the guy had been the donor's boyfriend. I didn't really find it very realistic but I do think sometimes very unrealistic things can happen.

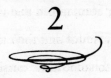

2

That night Mam was watching *Grey's Anatomy* and Dad was reading the paper beside her. How he could follow what he was reading was beyond me – Mam kept hitting his arm every two minutes and saying things like, 'I knew they'd get together' or 'Didn't I say it was probably her lungs?' or 'Good Lord I never saw that coming.'

I took advantage of their domestic bliss to look again for the perfume. To be honest it was the letters I wanted to find. But when I opened the drawer they were gone. I thought of asking Mam about them but I knew that was probably not a great idea. It wasn't as if I didn't know all about this Marie. I had known for six years. I just didn't think she was so much a part of Mam's life now.

When I was six, my mother and father sat me down in the living room and told me they wanted to have a chat about our family. That it was time to know a bit of the history.

I knew it was serious because they sat beside each other and across from me and were both smiling their heads off.

They started by telling me that they went to Dingle on their honeymoon. This I already knew and in fact Dad was always showing me pictures of Fungie the Dolphin who lives there and came right up beside them on the boat. The pictures just look like they are of waves to me but Dad always said, 'Look you can see him just under the water,' so I always pretended to see. After Dingle they went to Connemara and walked along the beach at

Lettermore. And that is where Mam saw an abalone shell for the second time in her life.

Abalone. A beautiful bluey-green shell that seems to change colours in the sun. The first time she saw abalone was on the dreamcatcher Aunt Kate had in Canada. And now there it was right on the beach in Connemara.

The Ojibwa Nation believed the dreamcatcher kept the spirit in harmony as it walked through Dreamland. Mam thought that sounded like a good idea and that if she ever got a dreamcatcher she would want to decorate it with a shell. She said it was just sitting there on a rock and the greeny-blue colour was what caught her eye. It wasn't the whole shell – just a tiny piece a little bigger than her thumbnail – but it looked exactly like a butterfly sitting on the rock. As she pocketed the perfect piece of shell, she felt like something special was happening. The next day she found out she was pregnant and she said they were over the moon and she decided to save the butterfly shell and give it to this child to mind him or her always.

A her as it turned out.

My sister.

Dad took over the story then and said, 'She was born on the 16th of April, she was perfect, and her name was Marie.'

I wanted him to keep going so I didn't ask any questions like, 'Isn't Marie my name??'

Marie only lived seven weeks. One morning Mam went to collect her from the cot and she wasn't there. Her little spirit had gone. Mam held her for hours waiting for it to come back. She said she kept willing her to come back. Hoping against hope. Checking every two minutes to see if maybe she had started breathing again. And when Dad found them sitting together in the rocking chair a few hours later, it took ages to convince Mam that Marie wasn't ever coming back. So they put her back in the cot and called the doctor to 'make arrangements'.

Then Mam started talking again and I was a bit frightened because I had never seen her cry before. And it wasn't normal crying – I mean there were tears coming down her cheeks but her voice was gentle like she was just explaining how to make muffins or something.

Mam said they dressed Marie in the tiniest blue and white dress that had pleats at the bottom and a tiny pocket near the top. 'Imagine. As if a baby needs a pocket,' she said. 'It was a very sad time for us but we had to accept that things don't always go to plan. I wanted to give Marie the beautiful butterfly shell when she got older but that wasn't meant to be, so I put it in the little pocket of the blue and white dress where it could be buried with her and near her heart forever.'

Dad said, 'And so the little pocket came in handy after all. Now I think we should all have some ice cream – to celebrate our family history.'

I wasn't really quite sure what we were celebrating but I guess it is a big deal to find out you have a sister even if she is dead. But to be honest I still felt like an only child.

While Dad was getting the ice cream Mam said she

wanted to show me something. She went over to the bookcase and reached behind a book and took down a beautiful little photo album with a pink satin cover. In it were pictures of Marie and my mam and dad. It was hard to see Marie's face or what she looked like because she was so small and she was always wrapped in a blanket or a towel or something. Dad kind of looked the same but Mam looked so different. For one thing she was really thin in the picture. I wanted to ask her, 'What happened? What made you change so much? Is this really you?' But I didn't say anything because she still seemed upset from talking about Marie. Then she put her arm around me and said it was exactly one year and two months after the funeral that something wonderful happened and they were over the moon again because she found out she was pregnant.

Pregnant with me.

And when I was born I got a dead baby's name.

Now I was Marie and she was the Other Marie.

The Other Marie. I liked the sound of it until Rachel used it. Then I felt embarrassed and I worried that somehow, thanks to Rachel, everyone was going to know our family secret.

3

Our religion teacher Miss Murphy was originally from Vermont, though you'd be hard pressed to find anyone with a more Dublin accent than her. Hard pressed. I like the sound of that. As if something was ironed so flat it would be impossible for anything to hide under it.

Miss Murphy was one of those teachers who tries a bit too hard. She was always smiling and saying everything was great. She wrote our first assignment on the board, 'What Autumn Means to Me', and we were all supposed to make or bring in something that has to do with autumn. Then she sounded all excited when she said, 'And girls, there may even be some pumpkin pie when we talk about the pilgrims and Thanksgiving.' Almost everyone was rolling their eyes when she gave us the assignment. I guess I should have realised that no one was going to make anything.

Religion is a class you can't really fail so I don't know why I worked so hard. I guess it's just that once I got started I kind of got into it. I decided to make a cape of leaves all different colours, like in the autumn. I had lots of coloured construction paper so my plan was to cut out leaves in red and yellow and orange and paste them on a cape that I cut out of a huge roll of paper we have. It's actually wallpaper lining but Dad said I can use it whenever I want.

I sat on the floor in my bedroom and cut and cut and I loved the clean sound of the scissors and soon I had a pile of leaves and I glued them on the paper and by the time

I finished it was really late so I only had time to scribble about two lines in my diary and then I went to bed.

Only a handful of people had bothered to do anything. There were a few drawings and a couple of people cut out stupid things from magazines but I was the only one who made something to wear. I looked like an idiot when I put on the cape in class.

Jill had a rubber turkey mask. I don't know where she got it but I have to admit it was fantastic. And Rachel couldn't stop going on about it. I made a joke to Rachel about how we should try and get Miss Murphy to try it on but she just looked right through me and asked Jill to pass the pumpkin pie which by the way wasn't as great as I thought it would be.

The next week we were going to be studying Hindi traditions but you could be sure I wasn't going to be doing anything stupid like making a costume again.

That night I almost asked Mam about Other Marie. I needed to know if she thought about her all the time. Is that why she wrote her letters? I didn't know how I was going to ask that without my perfume borrowing plan being revealed so I said nothing. Instead I read like I do every night.

I know it's a weird hobby to have but I like reading. I love that feeling of not being able to put a book down. I read until quarter to twelve with the torch under the covers – Mam would have killed me if she knew I was up that late.

I was reading a mystery about a detective who was searching for a killer and ended up finding his ex-girlfriend's bones in a wall and all along he thought she had just left him for someone else. Excellent. And it really helped me forget about school.

4

It was during our second Art class that Nicole knocked all the contents of my pencil case off my desk. It was so embarrassing. It happened as she went up to ask the teacher a question. She just swished by, swept them onto the floor and then looked all sympathetic as if was my fault. Bitch.

She was one of *them*. The Super Six they called themselves although I also heard that in private they called themselves the Sexy Six. Rachel, Nicole, Marie, Jill, Jade and Claire. They were all skinny – well except for Jade but maybe they just let her hang around with them so they looked even skinnier. They were obsessed with taking pictures of themselves with their phones even though you get your phone taken away for a week if you are caught using it in class or taking pictures anywhere on school property. They always had lunch together and, except for Marie from Poland who seemed to work very hard, they hardly ever did their homework and yet they managed to never get in trouble.

I *was* going to keep a file on everyone in the class but I didn't have time for that so I decided just to keep one on the Stupid Six.

*

Every now and then I had one of those rare days when I thought my hair actually looked presentable. This particular day I blow dried it as straight as I could and then combed through some leave-in conditioner and it actually took away the frizz. Then I put on the brown hairband that's just a shade lighter than my hair colour and I pulled a bit of hair out so I had some at the front and side. Mam said I looked gorgeous.

I think she was pleased I was wearing the hairband. I know it doesn't sound like a big deal but she bought it for me in Hickey's and like I said she hardly ever goes out. But she did on the weekend and she also got me a bag of Haribo sweet and sours.

At breakfast Dad showed me a cartoon from the newspaper that I didn't really get. I almost never get them but I pretend I do. That's always been our thing but I'm kind of tired of it and I don't know how to tell him. He said he loves having a daughter who is up on things. 'Half the people in work don't even read the paper. And they're supposed to be running the country.'

Dad works with the Department of Agriculture, Food and the Marine. He took me with him last year when he had to inspect some of the salmon fisheries in Galway. It was just the two of us and I got off school as well – not that missing school mattered in primary school. It was fun but things are different now and I told him I can't actually afford to take time off next week to visit the wind generators in Wexford. He didn't look a bit sad about it. He just said, 'Glad to see somebody takes their responsibilities seriously' which I think had something to do with the cartoon he had shown me but I can't be sure.

*

Mr McGuire said poems are meant to be read out loud so that's what we do in class. He always skips over Lucy Brennan so she doesn't have to read. She gets so many words wrong that you just have to laugh even though you know you shouldn't. Once we were reading an English short story and it was her turn to read out loud and she said *booby* instead of *bobby*.

The Stupid Six (who I am very sure don't know that

a bobby is an English policeman) couldn't stop laughing even after everyone else stopped. The next day when we got in someone (not hard to guess who) had written on the whiteboard, 'Loosie Brennan is a booby.' When Lucy came in she turned really red and almost started crying before going up to erase it. I think she was more upset about someone making fun of her name than about her mistake in reading because all she erased was the Loosie Brennan part. I also think Rachel is mean to her core.

Anyway that Tuesday – the day my hair actually looked presentable – we were doing a poem I really loved. It was about a man who nobody noticed except when he left down a bag and walked towards the harbour never to be seen again. And it all took place at an inquest investigating his death. And everyone says they didn't notice him. It's tragic and romantic at the same time.

After we finished reading it out loud Mr McGuire asked Rachel what she thought it was about. She said, 'Um Sir it's about living by the sea?'

Unfortunately he asked me next which I could tell really bugged Rachel. I said it was about the guilt people felt at not noticing someone and Mr McGuire smiled at me and said, 'Now we're getting somewhere.'

I was really happy he said that but then my neck felt hot which meant it was turning red so even though I was enjoying the class I was pretty glad that just then the bell went and class was over.

The next class was Religion and while Miss Murphy was showing us slides from her trip to India last summer with her husband, Stella started whispering something to me although I didn't realise it was me she was talking to because she often talks to herself and she rarely starts conversations in school.

Stella was quite unusual and even though no one really talked to her she didn't seem to mind when we asked her to play the phone game. We discovered the game by accident – Stella put her hands behind her back and someone put their phone or iPod in her hands and then she said what the make was and who it belonged to – without looking!

She acted like it wasn't anything special but of course no one else could do it. She never made a mistake, so when Hannah put a phone in her hand and Stella said, 'It's a Nokia 215 and because of the scratch at the side I think it's the one that was stolen from Jennifer's bag in Room 1A,' Hannah looked a bit sick. No one said anything but I did hear that Jennifer found her phone that very afternoon in the second floor bathroom.

Anyway Stella kept whispering to me during the slide-show until Miss Murphy said, 'Stella would you like to share your story with the class?'

And she said, 'I was just trying to tell Marie she has gum in her hair in her hair.'

And of course then everyone looked at me. Rachel actually said, 'Miss, maybe she slept with it in her mouth and it came out in the night. That happened to my cousin when she stayed with us last summer and she didn't know it was there and I'm sure Marie didn't know it was there.'

Of course I didn't know it was there and it didn't take a genius to figure out who was responsible for it getting there. I definitely saw Rachel looking at Jill and trying not to laugh. Miss Murphy said, 'Thank you Rachel for trying to make Marie feel better. You may be excused and come back when you're sorted Marie.'

Feel better?

Sorted?

I took my math set with me to the loo and I used the compass to cut the gum out of my hair. It took ages and I wished I had scissors but finally I got the gum out (and a chunk of my hair too) and folded it into a piece of paper with the date on it. Exhibit A.

Yes I'll have to get things sorted all right.

5

Right after the gum in the hair day it started.

I heard a baby crying at night. At first I thought it was a kitten. Then I thought I was dreaming and then suddenly I was wide awake and I knew it was a baby. My heart started beating really hard and I just lay there not moving a muscle. I tried to hear if Mam or Dad were getting up to see what was happening but I guess they didn't hear it. It sounded like the baby was in the house but I knew that wasn't possible. I lay there listening for ages and I don't know how I fell asleep but I guess I did because soon it was morning.

The next night it woke me again, and again I couldn't see anything – I could just hear a baby crying faintly like it was in my head or in a room somewhere and I felt too scared to get out of bed and look for it and soon my heart was beating so hard I couldn't hear anything and eventually I fell back to sleep. I waited for Mam or Dad to say something at breakfast about hearing it but they didn't say anything so neither did I.

At school after the third night of waking up and hearing the baby, we were doing a poem in class called 'Spirit Journey on a Hallow's Eve' and it hit me. Maybe it was Other Marie – trying to contact me. Maybe she had a message for me or maybe she just wanted me to make her feel better. I didn't tell Mam or anyone. I knew I would just sound crazy. I didn't believe in ghosts then. I wasn't scared – just tired. 'A broken sleep is worse than a short one,' Mam said. Broken is right but I said nothing.

The creepy thing is, that wasn't the first time I heard something crying when nothing was there. When I was ten we went to Kerry and while we were walking on White Strand beach in Caherciveen I told my mam I could hear a baby crying. Mam stopped still and didn't laugh just asked me what made me say that. And when I said, 'Can't you hear it?' she just smiled and said, 'You're a very sensitive girl Marie.'

My dad did an 'oh come on' sound with his breathing and just looked at my mam who said nothing. Then he tried to cheer her up by saying how well she was looking these days and it felt like they had forgotten I was there. But she didn't look well at all – she was getting so fat. Was I the only one who saw that?

On the way home in the car when Mam and Dad thought I was asleep Mam brought it up again. 'Seriously Frank, why would she say such a thing at that exact spot. That must be exactly where that baby washed up on shore.'

Then I was sorry I had pretended to be asleep because I wanted to say, 'What? Do you think I heard a ghost? Am I psychic?' But I didn't say anything and Dad changed the subject and pretty soon I really was asleep so I don't know if they said anything else about it.

*

I did some research on the Internet. There are millions of stories about hearing things in the night but none of them sounded like my experience and I don't really know what I was expecting anyway.

I went to the library like I did every Thursday and returned *The Girls of Virginia High* which I got out the week before. It was okay but the plot was really predictable – every single chapter ended with one of the girls crying about someone kissing her boyfriend.

I never saw anyone I knew at the library except come to think of it sometimes Stella was there – at the back sitting on one of those plastic chairs for little kids. She was usually by herself and drawing. I didn't know her very well then so I never said anything. I don't think she ever noticed me because her face was always about two inches away from the paper.

I got out *Wait Till Helen Comes* because it looked like it was about somebody coming back from the grave. The librarian smiled as if I was eight and said, 'I hope this doesn't keep you up at night.' If only she knew what did keep me up.

When I started reading it I kind of got the creeps so I had to put it down. The main girl Molly was twelve and wanted to be a writer and then her younger stepsister Heather who was seven found a tombstone of a girl who was seven when she died and had the same initials as her. Then when Heather started visiting the grave and talking to someone that no one else could see . . . that was when I had to put it down.

They had moved in next door to a graveyard which seems like a ridiculous thing to do so it was quite different from my experience. And it was fiction. What was happening to me was real. Anyway I put it down and reread *Watership Down* instead.

*

Superstitions aren't always something you can control. I don't mean that stepping on a crack will break my mother's back but sometimes I have to do weird things or something awful will happen. Somewhere I know this is very childish, but what if it does work? 'Better to be safe than sorry' is another one of my dad's sayings – though I'm very sure he doesn't mean do stupid things to keep safe. One of the things I did when people like Rachel and Claire were talking about me even though I was right there and I could hear them was try and write my name with my big toe inside my shoe. It gave me something to concentrate on and by the time I finished they usually had stopped. If they hadn't it was because I had forgotten to dot the *i* or something and so I started over.

The other thing I sometimes did was hold my Connemara stone. It's perfect and round and smooth and I found it on the beach near Lettermore. When I rub it three times and make three wishes one of those wishes should come true within three days. I use it a lot coming up to Christmas or my birthday.

The toe thing was all I could do when I was in school and it helped me feel like I was holding my breath so that when I stopped and Rachel and the others were finished tormenting me I could breathe again.

It was usually Rachel who would talk about me as if I was invisible. She'd say things like, 'Wow Other Marie is really looking gorgeous today. Her neck and face were a lovely red when Mr McGuire got her to read out loud.' And then the others would all laugh as if they were the funniest people they had ever met. I think the laughing was the worst part.

*

My mam is superstitious. She told me that a bird in the house means a death in the family. She also hates the colour green and once we got a gorgeous dark green couch delivered to the front room and Mam made the delivery men take it back. She told my dad, 'I'm sorry but I swear it looked blue in the shop.'

When I was ten a blackbird got into the house. It was flapping like crazy and crashing into the curtains as if it thought they were the door. Mam was waving a tea towel at it which only made it go more crazy. Finally it went out the open door and Mam looked like she was going to be sick. I didn't like it either but I did like how my heart was beating after. I could feel the blood going through my veins.

Mam didn't say anything. She was just sitting there with a weird look on her face and I heard Dad say, 'For God's sake Margaret, that's an old wives' tale. No one is going to die.'

But the next day Mam had to go into hospital and

Dad told me she had a miscarriage – I was supposed to have a baby brother or sister. But no one had told me and she didn't look pregnant although it would be hard to tell because she already looked fat but I didn't say that to Dad who looked quite sad. And that's when I learnt that sometimes superstitious things do come true.

When I asked Dad why they hadn't told me he said well she wasn't very far along. I didn't know for years what on earth that meant but I liked the sound and the feel of it – 'not very far along' – and I used to say it to myself when things weren't going well.

I couldn't wait for the Halloween break. I didn't care that I was too old to go trick or treating. I just wanted a break so I could start over. Maybe after the break things would be different. Maybe Rachel would decide she didn't hate me and then she and Jill would ask me to sit beside them and have lunch with them and talk about all the things we did over the break and then the baby crying at night would stop and I could get some sleep.

*

On the way home Stella was walking right behind me – so close that if I stopped she would crash into me. So I kind of waited and walked beside her. I wasn't crazy about having anyone see me walk beside her but I figured it would be a chance to ask her a few things. Like how come she escaped Rachel's evil eye – wasn't she way weirder than me? And why was she walking this way anyway? Didn't she live right across the street from the school?

But instead I asked her how she did the phone thing. And when she started to answer me she sounded different than she does at school. She still did the weird repeating thing every now and then but she sounded, I don't know, maybe smarter than I had thought.

She said it wasn't a trick, she was just more observant than most people and she had been born that way. She said she thought maybe she got her twin's observing genes. Her twin? Was she totally nuts? How could she have a twin and I hadn't noticed? I was so distracted thinking about this I kind of missed what she was saying – something about how it drove her crazy when her mother didn't get the blue uniform socks matching. 'They aren't all the same,' she said. 'You can feel the difference if you just listen to your hands to your hands.'

Okay. So she was a bit crazy.

I made up something about having to hurry to get home for an early dinner and I started to run and didn't look back.

I once read that identical twins can communicate telepathically, that even if they are separated at birth they are connected for life. There was one set of identical twins in Ohio who were adopted by different parents who named them the same name and then they grew up to marry girls with the same name and they even named their dogs the same name and they both became police officers. And then after thirty-nine years they were reunited and have been best friends ever since and live in identical houses right beside each other.

Maybe the twin thing is what protects Stella from Rachel. Or maybe Stella just hides things better than I do. I think Rachel isn't exactly the most patient person in the universe. It must really drive her crazy that Stella couldn't care less what she does. Maybe I'm too obvious. Mam always says I wear my heart on my sleeve but I thought that was a good thing. Anyway I'm not even sure that Stella has a twin. She doesn't strike me as a liar but it is pretty hard to believe she'd have one and no one would know about it.

6

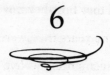

Today I got five anonymous texts. The first one said,

Well done in PE today. You should try out for the
basketball team

And although I didn't know who it was from as I don't
have anyone's number, it didn't take a genius to figure
out that it probably came from one of the Stupid Six.
All six of them spent PE sitting on the sidelines and had
notes because they were 'having their period'. How blind

can teachers be? How can they never see what is really going on?

It's not as if I did anything wrong in class. I wasn't the best but I certainly wasn't the worst. Gail threw the ball right at Miss Donnelly's head (I think on purpose) and everyone just laughed. Stella refused to run and no one seemed to be bugged by that. And I was totally normal. So much so that for one split second I thought the text might be real but then I saw Nicole and Rachel watching me when I read it and so I knew it wasn't. I didn't delete it because I wanted to remember the exact words when I put it in Rachel's file.

Then I read the other text which was from my dad and said,

hope today is better Dad x

He always signs his texts even though I've told him a million times his name comes up in my inbox. The text is an old one – from last week – but I like to keep reading it. He sent it to me the day after Other Marie started crying.

The next text came on my way home. It was from a different number and said,

> Luv your bag. Where did you get it?

I got three more that night. Three different numbers. Three carefully worded texts so that if I showed anyone they would say, 'Why Marie clearly someone wants to be your friend. Those are all compliments.'

> luv your hair you are so lucky you don't have to curl it

> do you want to have lunch with us?

> Mr McGuire loves you

I felt sick and kept reminding myself I wasn't very far along and soon it would be the Halloween disco and then the break and then a fresh start and then all this would be behind me.

*

The last day before the midterm break was the Halloween disco. The teachers made a big deal about it and the Principal announced it over the intercom. 'This is for the First Years only, so you girls can really get to know each other.'

Everyone kept saying this as if it were a good thing. As far as I could see everyone had already decided who they were interested in talking to (or tormenting).

And there weren't any boys allowed. It wouldn't have been that hard to arrange – I mean St Joseph's was just down the road and even though I didn't know anyone there and I would probably not have talked to any of the guys it would have been nice if Rachel and the Stupid Six were not the centre of attention for a change.

Anyway it was going to be fancy dress with prizes for the most inventive costumes. Unfortunately I should have known that what I think is inventive is probably way off what everyone else thinks. I wanted to wear something original but not too elaborate and I'd been dying to wear the present Dad gave me so I decided to go as a rooster weather vane.

Dad brought back this amazing hairband one time he went to a meeting in London. It was like those Christmas hairbands with antlers except it was a rooster sitting on an arrow and it was on a swivel so it kept swinging around. I thought I'd go simple for the rest of the outfit since the hairband was really the costume so I wore my red sweatpants and red long-sleeved T-shirt which would have been fine except the rooster thing came off the hairband on the way so it just looked like I was wearing red clothes. Four people asked me if I forgot my costume.

Stella came dressed as a fortune-teller. It wasn't a great costume – just a cape and a big glass ball. The ball was actually a snow globe and I couldn't believe it when I looked close: it had two pretend goldfish dressed as people, one was sitting in a deckchair and the other was sweeping and when you shook it it filled with snow.

Rachel was a glamour witch which meant she wore fishnet tights, her sister's high heels and a very tight black top with the top three buttons undone and a silver streak sprayed in her hair. She looked gorgeous. The majority of the girls were wearing tutus and had teased hair and lots of make-up.

I definitely misinterpreted the whole costume thing.

The Hall looked really good. The girls from Sixth Year had it all decorated with witches and spiders and big webs hanging down everywhere and little fairy lights in orange were hung around the doors. The music was also run by the Sixth Years so it was pretty good too.

Rachel was the one who decided that everyone should get their fortune told by Stella. It was really loud in the Hall so she told everyone to get in a line in the corridor beside the downstairs bathroom and that she would go first. Really her bossiness knows no bounds.

Stella acted as if this was just what she expected she'd be doing which is kind of how she reacts to everything. Rachel sat on a chair beside Stella in the corner so only she could hear. When she got up to give someone else a turn she was still smiling but walked away really quickly.

Even some of the teachers got in on it and when Miss Gilligan our geography teacher took a turn she got up and turned to us saying, 'Now come on girls enough of this nonsense,' and tried to hoosh everyone away. I waited for Stella who was still sitting in her chair looking at her goldfish. I went and sat beside her and she started shaking the ball and holding it to her ear and then she looked at me and said, 'Do you ever hear things that aren't really there?'

I got goosebumps on the back of my neck. I mean why would Stella say that? How could she know about the baby? But before I could ask her what she meant, Miss

Gilligan marched over and said, 'Put down that globe and start enjoying yourself girls.'

I didn't enjoy myself by the way but I did feel like something important had happened. I had never thought of Stella as friend material but I kind of liked her strangeness and how she didn't care what people thought about her. And I couldn't wait to talk to her again.

I went to the loo where I heard Rachel telling Jill that she saw Miss Gilligan crying and talking to Miss Murphy about 'being found out by Stella Fitzgibbon and what would happen to her marriage'.

Then Rachel noticed I was there and whispered to Jill that I was wearing red because I was having my period, and Jill laughed and said, 'Oh my God, that's so funny, let's go tell everyone.'

So I went home even before the sausage rolls were brought out. And if that wasn't bad enough, I got in trouble for walking home on my own instead of calling my dad to pick me up.

One good thing about the Stupid Six was that they didn't usually manage to remember who they were making fun of from one day to the next so I hoped that when we went back to school after the break they would have forgotten about my costume disaster.

I finished *Wait Till Helen Comes*, and the rest of it was very good and quite scary. It turned out Helen is the ghost of a girl who died in a fire a hundred years ago and she tries to lure Heather to her death and finally Molly saves her even though she doesn't really like her. Finally they bury the bones of Helen's parents so her spirit can rest. Like I said – fiction.

7

I really wished Other Marie would stop crying. It seemed to be getting worse. One night I woke to find myself looking for her in the bathroom and I wasn't sure how I got there. Mam was beside me and just said, 'There, there, let's go back to bed,' and that's all I remember. She didn't mention it the next morning so I said nothing. The longer I can keep it a secret that Other Marie's spirit is trying to contact me the better.

The break didn't start off all that well. Dad had to

work, and Mam didn't want to go anywhere. Twice I walked by Stella's house and once she was at her window just staring out at the sky so any thoughts of maybe calling on her went right out of my head I can tell you.

Instead I worked very hard on my book report which was on the diary of Anne Frank. At the end of the report I kept on writing as if Anne had continued to keep her diary in the concentration camp after she was arrested. I hoped Mr McGuire wouldn't think I was showing off. It just came easily as if she was talking to me herself even though she's dead and I know that's impossible. At the back of my copy of *The Diary of a Young Girl* there was a photograph of her actual diary. It was quite small with a red and white plaid cover and a little clasp to keep it closed. My diary is just a notebook with a pink cover. I'm kind of tired of it but there are still lots of pages to go before I can start a new one. Anyway I'm sure Anne Frank never complained about her cover so I won't either.

Then on the Thursday just as I was going to try and update my files, Stella came to my door and rang the bell. I don't know how she knew where I lived and she didn't even act like it was weird she just said, 'What are you doing doing?'

So I told her I was updating my files. I figured that would sound like something private and important but she just said she could help if I liked. I knew my mam was on the phone to Aunt Kate which meant Stella wouldn't have to see her so I said okay even though I had no intention of showing her my files which to be honest were pretty slim at this point and barely deserved to be called files.

Here's all I had so far.

Name: Rachel Quinn

- Her older sister had her picture taken with no shirt on when she was drunk last year and it's on Facebook.

- Deborah and Bea said they heard that Rachel's

dad doesn't always live with them.

- She lied that she had a boyfriend last summer just because Nicole really did have one.

I hate her hair and how thin she is and I hate how the teachers think she is so nice. Maybe they wouldn't like her so much if they knew what kind of family she comes from.

Name: Marie Krysinski

- Her mam can't speak English at all.
- Last year she was caught shoplifting some eye make-up.
- She's the one who put the gum in my hair.

Name: Jade Malone

- Rachel only likes her because her mam gets a discount at H&M because she works there.
- Rachel spread a rumour that she was throwing up after lunch in the bathroom.

- She won't eat anything white.

Name: Jill Patterson

- Last summer she and her brother drowned a kitten on purpose.

(Although Rachel is the one who said this in front of the class when Jill was out one day last week. And Rachel is definitely not to be trusted.)

- She can't really read very well.
- Her brother goes to a special school.

Name: Claire Flynn

- I don't think she likes Rachel.
- Last week she stole five euro from Rachel's purse and said that Jennifer Golding did it.

Name: Nicole Brennan

- She cheated on her Maths test before the break. She was sitting behind Jade and I saw Jade move

her paper to the side of her desk so she could
see it.
- She's the one who keeps pushing my pencils off
the desk.
- She had a boyfriend last summer which makes
Rachel very jealous.

I wasn't even sure if it was a good idea to keep these
files but if one day they all got arrested for some crime
against humanity maybe they would be useful evidence.

When Stella came in she asked if she could see my
room which felt a bit forward but I didn't really care so
I said okay.

She said, 'You have a lot of books. I collect shells collect
shells.' It wasn't as if that was a great conversation opener
so I figured I would be direct and just ask her what did
she mean when she said to me at the Halloween disco did
I hear things that weren't there.

She told me that sometimes I turned my head in school

as if I had heard something and that she used to do that when she was younger. Sometimes she would hear things really intensely – like the rustling of scarves was way too loud and the opening of books or people writing with pencils would make huge noises that she couldn't turn down. And then the next day it wouldn't be sounds any more it would be that everything she saw was too bright or too full of detail. She said she used to see all the veins on all the leaves on every plant on the way to school and that's why she used to go slowly – not because there was something wrong with her motor skills – as her parents had thought at the time.

So okay I guess she wasn't talking completely normally but she *was* making sense. I was a little disappointed she wasn't psychic but she was really clear about that: she said there was nothing about her that science couldn't explain. She was just observant and if you are really, really observant you notice things that other people don't.

I made a mental note not to ever tell her about the crying I heard because she clearly wasn't into the unexplained.

I really wanted to ask about her twin but she suddenly jumped up and said she had to go and thanks for everything.

After she left I was thinking about what she said about being observant and it reminded me of what Dad says: 'Marie, you have to keep an eye out for the little things. The human brain is capable of so much if we'd only really use it.' He also says we can develop our powers of observation and that most of the guys who bill themselves as magicians have done just that.

I'm not sure how that explains how Derren Brown can know everything about people he has never met. One woman in the audience of the show we were watching on TV the Friday before the break nearly had a heart attack she was so amazed when Derren said, 'Have you recently had an extension to your house and do you have relatives staying with you from far away – I'm getting the letter A – Australia?' The woman in the audience had tears running down her face as she said, 'Yes we did the extension from the money my dead brother left me and his son just arrived from Australia this afternoon!' I don't know how he knew that.

I really liked the experiment he did where he staged a robbery and then put people into a trance so they could remember the details of what they saw. And even people who said they didn't notice anything suddenly remembered the logo on the thief's shirt.

This skill would have come in so handy when I was doing my files. Usually by the time I got home I was too tired to fill them in – mostly because of my broken sleeps – and when I did get to them I couldn't remember what to write and they were all a bit vague and not that interesting.

8

I was kind of glad Stella had called on me even though she didn't stay long. I hardly ever have people come to the house. When I was in primary school my mam thought it was because I was shy but really it was because I thought there was something wrong with our house. It was too quiet, like not enough people lived in it.

I can always hear my mam and dad talking about me and there is never enough noise or colour in the air. I like my bedroom though. We have three bedrooms: one is

Mam and Dad's, one is mine and one is the guest room. That's the one that used to be Other Marie's room when she was alive.

Mam said it used to have yellow and white striped wallpaper and a white rocking chair and a little white dresser but she got rid of everything after Marie died and now it looks completely different. It sort of looks like a hotel room now – nice but always very tidy. One wall is maroon and the rest are white and the duvet on the bed is maroon and the lamp beside the bed has a maroon shade and it's all very matchy if you know what I mean. Aunt Kate and Uncle Dan stay there when they visit from Canada and so does Uncle Brian when he comes on business.

My bedroom is a tiny bit smaller but I like it. The walls are light blue and the blind is blue with white clouds on it and I have two bookshelves – one at the end of the bed and one beside the wardrobe. I don't want to give away my books – even the babyish ones. Mam keeps saying we should give the old ones to Oxfam but I sometimes reread the easy ones when I don't have anything good to read or when I feel a bit sick or nervous. I know that's a bit childish so I just tell her I'm sentimental and can't part with them yet and that usually stops her saying anything about Oxfam for a few months. I have a chair and a desk by the window too – that's where Stella sat when she came.

I used to have lots of things on the wall like photographs from holidays and tickets from the plane we took to visit Canada last summer and pictures of seals from when I was in my Save the Seal phase and class pictures, but I took them all down. I thought I would try for a more minimalist look now that I'm in secondary school. There are bits of Blu-Tack stuck to the walls from where I took things down which I kind of like but Mam keeps telling me to take off. What I also like about my room is that Dad hung a light on the wall beside my bed and I hardly have to reach to turn it off at night when I finish reading.

I think Mam wishes I would have more people over. I heard her say to Dad she thought I had gone into myself ever since the confirmation, but that wasn't really true. I think the whole confirmation thing bothered her more than it bothered me although it did bother me a bit.

Last year, in Sixth Class, a boy called Hossein and I were the only ones not making our confirmation. I didn't make my communion either but we went to Cork at the same time as that was happening so I don't really remember much about it except that when I got back everyone seemed to have loads of money.

But confirmation was different. The teacher never stopped talking about what a big deal it was and about how it set you apart from the others and how you would then be a soldier of Christ which she definitely made sound like you would be better than everyone else. She said all this in front of me and Hossein as well. And he was one of the nicest boys in the class.

Mam and Dad said I could get new clothes and we would all go to the church but Dad was very firm when I suggested maybe I could do my confirmation too. I was actually wondering what it would feel like to be a soldier of Christ even if it was only for a day. But he said, 'No, you won't be taking part Marie because confirmation is for Catholics and you aren't even baptised not to mention it would be hypocritical to pretend to be a Catholic for that one day. Even though I've no doubt that's what some of your classmates will be doing.'

The actual ceremony was a bit boring but Dad let me use his video camera because I wanted to record it and I almost had a heart attack when I thought I had cracked the camera when I sort of dropped it on the pew when we were sitting down. I was trying to figure out how much babysitting I'd have to do to replace it when Dad asked for it and I had to give it to him. He said, 'Good Lord I don't know how you could see anything with this hair over the lens – I thought it was a crack at first.' I was so relieved it was a hair and not a crack that I completely enjoyed the rest of the ceremony even though it did seem to go on for ever.

Because we were sitting behind the class I could see the boys hitting each other on the arm when they thought no one was looking. I couldn't believe how many people's phones went off. Dad said it was probably because they were the types who never went to church except for weddings or communions or confirmations. I'm not sure why he got so worked up about it.

The priest hardly seemed to notice although it really drove our principal Mrs Byrne mad. She started doing the really tight mouth thing she did whenever she was angry in Assembly. Which was all the time by the way.

So, the Confirmation Day itself wasn't really the problem. It was the following Monday when Mrs Byrne announced there would be a gathering in the Hall for the confirmation class – only those who had made their confirmation would attend. The rest of the class (which meant just me since Hossein was out that day) would spend that time in the computer room.

It turned out that the 'gathering' was a party. No

prayers or anything, just sweets and crisps and cans of Coke. I was very surprised when Anthony and Sam, who I don't even know that well, separately managed to sneak out of the party and bring me some crisps and Coke. I think Anthony did it because he wanted to see if he could do it without getting caught. I think Sam did it because he felt sorry for me. I didn't care why – I thought it was nice.

But I wouldn't have said anything about the party to my parents if I thought they were going to make such a big deal about it. The next day my mam went storming into the school to talk to Mrs Byrne. I overheard her telling Dad about it: 'I told that woman in no uncertain terms that no child should be excluded from a party. A party for God's sake! The board is going to hear about this.'

After that there was just one month until the end of school so I tried not to think about it. I got my silent revenge by never looking at Mrs Byrne in the eyes again.

Even when she addressed me I'd look at her face but just beside her eyes or just over her shoulder. I'm pretty sure she hated that but she wasn't the kind of person who really showed what she was feeling so who knows.

The class photograph that year was actually of the confirmation class which meant I wasn't in it which was one of the reasons I took down everything from my wall.

*

The nights were getting worse. Once I woke up and heard Other Marie crying and it sounded like she was under my bed. I sort of held my breath and just lay perfectly still even though I really wanted to call out for Mam and finally she stopped or I went to sleep I'm not sure which. Another time I heard her just before I fell asleep and that was the scariest of all. Was she going to start taking over my waking hours as well? That only happened once. The rest of the times I woke in the middle of the night and sometimes I was awake for ages. I was so tired.

*

The only problem with having a midterm break is that you have to have a first day again. It was a bit worse than the real first day because now I knew what to expect. The teachers didn't call me Other Marie, but it seemed that no one else had forgotten about that over the break and when I came in to school Rachel said, 'Oh hi Other Marie – or should I just say O.M.?'

Cue lots of ridiculous laughter from the five morons who surrounded her.

In English I sat where I always sat but then Claire and Jade moved at the same time so there was a big space beside me.

Stella sat at the very back but she always put a red pencil on the chair in front of her and an orange one behind her so no one would sit in front or behind her. Apparently the sides didn't matter. And not once did anyone move the pencils or try to sit near her. The meanest anyone ever got (and almost everyone did this) was people said, 'Hi Stella Stella.' And she would say, 'Hi hi' as if it was the most normal thing in the world.

When I realised that nothing had changed I tried very hard not to cry and I picked at a scab on my knee under the desk to distract me. I cut my knee when we went to Sandymount Strand the first Sunday of the break and I fell on the beach racing my dad back to the car. It was quite sore when it happened. Bits of shell and seaweed were stuck in the cut and I didn't take them out till I got home. I sort of wanted to make a spectacular entrance. And it worked. Mam was very concerned and started throwing Dettol at it saying, 'Frank, for goodness sake why don't you go to the bakery and get some éclairs or something?'

I was in the middle of nearly getting the scab off when Mr McGuire came in and said, 'Now. About the book reports.' Suddenly lots of girls started panicking and flinging their arms in the air saying, 'Sir, Sir, I left mine at home' or, 'Sir, Sir, mine is finished but I was going to print it out but we ran out of ink.'

'Sir, Sir.'

And Mr McGuire being the understanding gentleman and best teacher this school has ever seen in my opinion (although to be fair I don't really know that many teachers as I'm only in First Year) said, 'Relax girls – you have until Friday to get it in which you would know if you had written the due date in your journals. What I was going to say was, would anyone who is finished like to read theirs out loud?' Then he looked at me and I felt my neck and face go red and without even realising what I was doing I put up my hand. I knew everyone would hate me for being finished but it didn't seem like things could get much worse on that front. I was also a bit worried that someone would notice my knee with the half picked scab and think it was gross. But by the time I got to the ending – the part which if I do say so myself almost brought tears to my eyes – I noticed it was very quiet in the room, a listening quiet. Then everyone clapped. Really clapped. Not with big woo-hoos like when someone popular does something and everyone wants to get away from doing real work so they get kind of carried away – just real clapping. As if they thought it was good. Though I know it would be going too far to say it was as if they liked me.

Never underestimate the power of the written word for that lunchtime was the first time Rachel asked me if I wanted to go with them to the canteen. At our school you can either eat your lunch in your base room or in the room with the long tables and the vending machines that everyone calls the lunchroom. One of the machines is filled with bottled water and Nutri-Grain bars and the other has chocolate Wagon Wheels, Wine Gums, Skittles, Crunchies, Cokes, Diet Cokes, Fantas and Lucozades. I'll let you guess which machine gets more business. I actually like Nutri-Grain bars but I never buy them there because Mam buys them in bulk to put in my lunchbox.

Rachel made a big deal of saying, 'Sit here beside me Marie.'

I should have known something was up when she didn't call me Other Marie but I was so pleased I didn't see the signs. Rachel's lunch consisted of a Wagon Wheel and a Lucozade, and she thought it was cute that I was eating an egg salad sandwich from home. Then she got to the point. Since I was so good at writing how would I like to do her English homework for her and to make it sound like she had written it. She would copy it in her own handwriting before handing it in. In exchange I could go with them to Dundrum Town Centre on Friday after school.

For one thing, I probably wouldn't be allowed to go to Dundrum Town Centre and if I was I wouldn't have any money to buy anything. But more importantly than that it felt like cheating and I wanted no part of it so I said, 'I don't think so.'

You should have seen her face. She kept smiling and was all nicey nice and said, 'Oh, all right.' But as we were getting ready to go to class she said very very quietly so only I could hear, 'You'll be sorry.' And the way she said it made me feel sorry already and I knew then I had made a terrible mistake. But I didn't know how to fix it because she was off with her entourage surrounding her on the way to Geography.

After school when I went to use the bathroom Nicole and Claire were in there and they stopped talking as soon as I came in and just stared at me and then they were silent until I went into the cubicle and then they started whispering and laughing their heads off and I know it was about me. How I looked or something I said or maybe Rachel had told them I said no and they were plotting some revenge.

When I got to my locker Rachel was leaning against it and talking to Jade and even though both their lockers are way down at the end of the hall they stayed there for ages and when I said, 'Excuse me,' they acted like I was invisible.

When I got home I wanted to go straight to bed I was so tired of it all. Instead I started my Home Ec homework. We had to make a display of different stitches on a piece of coloured felt.

I don't even know why I did it but I sort of scratched my arm accidentally on purpose with the needle and it felt awful and good at the same time. I knew it wouldn't leave a scab because it was so light so I did it again deeper and although it hurt I felt like I could breathe again. It reminded me of when I felt the blood coursing through my veins the day the bird was in our house.

That night was the first night in ages I didn't hear Other Marie and so I slept through and when I woke up I didn't dread going to school – I felt like there was something to look forward to even if I couldn't remember what it was. Then I checked my arm and remembered. The scab would be perfect for picking at if things didn't go well in school. Mam asked me in a worried voice if I had slept well and I said, 'Yes fine,' and had two waffles for breakfast which seemed to take the worry out of her eyes.

*

Thank God I had the cut is all I can say because Rachel was in full swing. It started when I came to my locker and the six of them stared and stared at me until I got my books and went into class.

Most of that day I tried not to notice the staring and the blocking me in the halls. I pretended I didn't care. In Religion class I started picking at the cut and it felt good and I didn't really hear what was going on in class but the time flew and soon it was time for English.

We weren't supposed to have our phones on in school but absolutely everyone – even Stella I bet – had theirs on silent or at least turned them on between classes to check them for texts. Usually my texts were hellos from Dad but that day I got one from an unknown number.

> think I'll forward lovely picture of you that I have
> to Mr McGuire

For a minute I felt sick but I'm not a complete idiot. I knew it was probably from Rachel and she has never taken a picture of me as far as I know and also she couldn't possibly have Mr McGuire's number and even if she did she would hardly send a text from her phone knowing it could be traced.

But still I felt embarrassed which I'm sure was Rachel's plan all along. Well done Rachel. Bull's eye. My neck and face were hot which meant I was blotchy and red so I didn't answer any of the questions even though I really liked the short story we were doing which is called 'The Gift', all about a sick boy who gets to meet his football hero.

*

Before I started at St Bridget's Mam said, 'An all-girls school will be a great place to make friends. If you use half the energy you put towards your reading and spend it trying to make friends I'm sure you will meet some lovely girls.' She doesn't get that when I'm reading I don't feel stupid – there's no chance of getting things wrong.

At school I seemed to get even the simplest things wrong and when I did Rachel always managed to be there. I did my best not to show anything but she seemed to know when indeed she had hit a bull's eye. I know if I told anyone the things she did they would just think I was crazy so I said nothing and read.

*

That night after I did my own homework, I just lay on my bed and looked at all my old books. I almost picked up a Famous Five book to read but instead I started thinking about how Enid Blyton must have had so much fun imagining she was those kids on adventures. I wondered if I could do that, and so I picked up my pen and pretended I was Rachel and I did the homework again, making the kind of mistakes I thought Rachel might make. It was really easy.

When I finished that I scraped my arm again with the needle and again that night Other Marie did not wake me and although I was relieved I sort of missed her and hoped I would hear from her again.

The next day I could feel the cuts on my arm sort of throbbing. Stella kept staring at the spot just above my elbow on my left arm. I knew she couldn't actually see through my jumper and she couldn't have known about the cuts but she is very observant and I felt like she knew. Is that possible?

We had a spare class before English so I folded the A4 pages with Rachel's homework and put them on her desk. She picked them up and smiled at me and said, 'Thanks,' like she knew I was going to do them so I felt kind of confused and I didn't say anything.

I knew Stella was looking at me so I kept my eyes down. I felt like I had sold my soul and even though I thought everything would be better because then Rachel would like me, I knew it would actually be worse and the rest of the day I didn't look at anyone.

When I was walking home Rachel drove by in her

mam's fancy car and she rolled down the window and said, 'Bye Marie. See you tomorrow,' in the suckiest voice imaginable.

I would have loved to send an anonymous text to her mother – to let her know just what her perfect daughter really was like. But here's the weird thing: even though I knew she was being fake, I was kind of happy Rachel had talked to me.

That night – not because I was upset but because I felt good – I cut my other arm, up high so it wouldn't show even when I was wearing the short-sleeved gym shirt.

9

I got a book out of the library called *Poltergeists and Other Mysteries of the Paranormal*. Some of it was a bit hard to understand but the part I did get said that most poltergeists are actually girls my age who can move things around really quickly so that no one notices. So it isn't really a ghost in the house, more like it's a girl who has gone a bit crazy.

I found this fascinating but not that helpful as I was more interested in finding out about people making contact from the other side. I was sure Other Marie had some kind of message for me. Or maybe there is a completely scientific explanation for what is happening. I wanted to ask Stella because even though I was sure she didn't believe in ghosts she would probably listen to me without laughing and more importantly without telling anyone. But there never seemed to be the right time.

*

Every Thursday night I did Rachel's composition for her and every Friday I folded it and put it on her desk. And every Friday Stella watched but didn't say anything. Rachel never said anything either. She never mentioned going to Dundrum Town Centre with them. My only thanks seemed to be that she didn't always call me Other Marie. I knew I should just stop doing her homework but I kind of enjoyed pretending I was someone else and besides if I stopped, Rachel would do something. I just knew it.

Mam and Dad kept asking me if everything was okay

and I just lied and said of course and tried to sound really cheerful. Up until then I never lied, apart from the time I stole gum when I was six and my bright idea for hiding it from my dad was putting the entire packet in my mouth, insisting there was nothing in my mouth and then (when there seemed no escape from the reality of the gum's existence) insisting I had bought it with my own money. But I was only six so it hardly counts.

Now lying was getting to be second nature to me. After asking me if everything was okay, Dad usually said, 'Tell us – what did you learn today that you didn't know yesterday?' So I told them amusing anecdotes based on just enough truth to keep me going. It was getting exhausting, but I figured it was good practice for when I became a published writer.

I told them how nice Samantha was and how she asked me to call her Sammy and how her aunt has a horse on her farm in Mayo and how she asked me to go with her next summer to visit. Completely making someone up seemed like a good idea at the time but I hadn't really thought it through and then they wouldn't stop talking about her and would I like to have her over. I was going to have to make her move or something.

After that I more or less stuck to the truth but made it all sound like lots of fun. I couldn't believe they believed me. I told them things like 'Art was really fun – we made pen and ink drawings of our favourite animals' when in fact we *did* do pen and ink drawings and they *were* of our favourite animals but 'really fun' is about as far away from the truth as you could get.

When Sister Pauline left the room Claire and Marie took out their phones and started taking pictures of each other and then they said they were going to take pictures of our art and put the best ones on Facebook with our names under them. My picture was okay – a sort of lying down dog, a cocker spaniel which is the most gorgeous of dogs I think.

Then Rachel said, 'Oh that's so good.' She sounded

like she meant it and for a minute I thought, 'Oh no please don't ask me to do your art for you as well,' but all she said was, 'Why don't you sign it?' and when I went to sign it Jill just 'happened' to bump my elbow and the ink just 'happened' to blob on top of the dog and then Sister Pauline came back.

Her shoes are so noisy you can hear her coming for miles so everyone was in their seats and working away when she arrived back.

And then – this is the worst part – I started to cry. I really couldn't help it. I told Sister Pauline I had allergies and could I please be excused and so I was.

On my way out I saw Stella's picture and it was fantastic. Mind you, you wouldn't have known the assignment was to draw an animal as nearly every inch of the paper was covered with flowers. Even though they were black and white they looked so real I couldn't believe it. There was an extremely small cat in the corner so technically she followed the instructions. Anyway I doubted she'd end up on Facebook as the Stupid Six acted like she hardly existed which in my opinion was a lucky thing.

*

One Saturday I asked Mam if we could go to Nutgrove Shopping Centre and it turned out that was a big mistake. Mam doesn't like going shopping because she is so fat but I thought if she got some new clothes she might feel better. The Warehouse has really regular clothes and I was pretty sure she could find something that fit her and maybe I could get something new as well. Now if I had been completely honest with my mam about the shopping I would have said, 'I am 99 per cent sure that no one I know will be there which really is the main reason I suggested Nutgrove.' I never in my wildest nightmare scenario imagined I'd run into Rachel.

Mam was looking through the sweatpants when I heard Rachel's stupid laugh. The sweatpants were right near the door and Rachel was with a gorgeous girl who looked about two years older than her. When she saw me she said in a loud oh we are such good friends voice, 'Marie! What are you doing here? The shops have absolutely nothing here. We had to come here because my cousin is visiting and we have to pick up chocolates because we're on our way to my aunt's and we totally forgot to get something to bring but why are you here?'

And unlike in school where she never talked to me or cared what I said, she was actually waiting for an answer when Mam called me. It was only when I heard Mam's voice calling me that I knew I didn't want Rachel to see her – to see how fat she was. So I didn't answer Mam and thankfully Rachel's gorgeous cousin said, 'Come on, we'll be late,' and off they went, and Mam came over to me just as I saw Rachel look back at us before turning the corner at the formal dress shop. She just looked at me and smiled. I'm not sure which was worse – that smile or me not wanting to be seen with Mam but ever since then I had real trouble getting to sleep.

✳

Sometimes I cut myself, and that helped for a bit, and then I tried to think up different stories I could write, and sometimes that distracted me but the sick feeling in my stomach wouldn't go away. Sometimes I heard Other Marie crying and woke up only seconds after finally getting to sleep. I was so tired the next day I could hardly get out of bed. And while I brushed my teeth I looked at the calendar of 'Lighthouses around the World' that Dad gave me last year, and I counted the days till Christmas break.

Two more Fridays.

Two more essays for Rachel.

*

The day before the Christmas holidays Stella came up to my locker and said, 'Do you want to come to my house my house? I'd like to show you something something.' The way she talked still made me kind of nervous. But I wanted to go, so after school we walked to her house and she didn't say a word on the way. When we got there we went straight to her bedroom which was a sort of lime green colour – not a bit bedroomy but sort of nice too.

To get into the room you had to step over her row of shells. She'd been collecting them since she was eight and she had them lined up on the floor up against the walls around the whole room and on the edge of the windowsill and on the edge of her bookshelf and even across the doorway so you had to step over them to get into the room.

She made a big deal before we went into her room about not moving anything anything. Stella said it wasn't that her brother Pete went in her room that bothered her – which by the way sounded like a perfectly normal thing to get mad at – but it was the moving of things even by one inch that bugged her. I didn't ask why. I figured it was just another Stella thing so I tried not to move anything even by one inch as I sat on her bed.

Then out of the blue she said, 'I know you think I'm crazy but I really did have a twin. It was a brother and he died in the womb when we were seven months old because he didn't have enough room.' Even though that was a very sad thing to hear, I suddenly felt really happy, like I had found a soulmate – someone who also had a dead sibling. I was about to give her a hug or say 'Oh sorry to hear that wait till I tell you about my dead sister and how she haunts me at night,' but suddenly Stella was gone from the room. When she came back she said, 'I'll show you something I don't usually show people and I have to ask you to swear not to tell anyone about it because I don't want people to think I'm weird.'

I almost said, 'People already think you are weird,' but that would have been mean so I said, 'Okay, swear.'

Then she showed me a white bag that looked like a make-up bag but in it was a needle and some liquid in a small jar. I'll say this about Stella: for someone who has weird social skills she can be very interesting. And before I knew it she was telling me about the time she almost died – when they first realised she was allergic to peanuts.

She was four and at a birthday party of a boy who lived next door. His name was Keith which was the name her mam said they would have called her brother if he lived. 'Synchronicity,' said Stella.

I pretended I knew what that meant but I had to look it up in the dictionary and now it is one of my favourite words though it's quite hard to slip it into everyday conversation. It means 'the coincidence of events that seem related but are not obviously caused one by the other.'

Anyway back to the near death experience. At the party Stella ate something – she says it was a chicken nugget but her parents say it was a peanut butter and chocolate brownie and her face literally turned blue in seconds. Apparently she's allergic to peanuts and even if she just gets a whiff of them her throat swells and she has twenty minutes to get to a hospital or she'll die. So they called an ambulance and on the way to the hospital she got an injection that stopped the swelling and now she has to carry this everywhere with her in case she comes across some peanuts.

I asked her if someone had been eating peanut butter and then kissed her would that count. Stella said she didn't know but maybe. She said they are developing pills that will work as well but so far she hasn't had them. And nothing has happened to her since she was four.

I was glad Stella didn't think my kissing question was stupid. The whole near death by peanuts story was so dramatic that I forgot to say anything about her twin or tell her about Marie.

When I was leaving she said, 'I sometimes think my parents must see a murderer when they look at me.' I wasn't exactly sure what she was talking about so I just said, 'I doubt that,' and Stella kind of smiled so I guess that was the right thing to say.

10

Every year we go to Connemara for Christmas and I love it. I have four cousins and an aunt and uncle and their house is very messy and I love it. Mam and Aunt Sinead talk for hours in the kitchen, and Dad and his brother Brian go for walks although I think they actually just walk to the village to go to the Red Fox which is a pub with a pool table that I am sometimes allowed to play on if it's before 5 o'clock.

Mam was worried about me. I heard her saying to

Aunt Sinead, 'She isn't herself and I can't get her to talk to me about it and she isn't sleeping at night.' And before I could hear any more my cousins came tearing through the hall where I was trying to eavesdrop. My cousins Sean and Darren are eight years old and they look so much alike that they make me wish I was a twin.

I wondered if Marie would visit me in Connemara. Do ghosts know where you are? Could she see me or did she only have a connection to our house because that was where she lived?

The other cousins are girls – Mairead, who is almost a year younger than me, and Gemma, who was nineteen months old although I don't get why they didn't just say she was a year and a half. Babies are hard enough work without having complicated ways of keeping track of their ages.

There was a baby down the road from them who Aunt Sinead said was sixteen weeks old. Then she said he was twenty-four inches long which gave me no idea of what he looked like till we saw him and he looked like a normal baby, though as for how many inches he was who could tell as he had about four blankets on him and a hat and a jacket with a hood. No wonder they don't do much at that age.

Mairead is amazing and although she is a year younger than me, when it comes to outdoor age she's a million times older and smarter. For one thing she was allowed to go anywhere she wanted. I could barely go into town without being interrogated about what bus and exactly what time, and Dad would meet me at the bus stop to walk me home even when it wasn't dark. Everyone in my class was allowed to do way more. And much and all as I love my parents I do think they are stuck in a time warp and don't have a clue what the real world is like.

When Mairead said, 'We're going to the second hill with Brunt,' I couldn't believe that the only thing her mam said was, 'Be back for dinner and take a light with you.'

Brunt was the most gorgeous sheep dog in the world and I think he really liked me. When we arrived he went crazy jumping on me and didn't even look at Mam or Dad which was a good thing as they probably wouldn't have been mad about him jumping all over them.

So off we went. Mairead was like a mountain goat and I was so happy not to be worrying about what to wear or say that I sort of started crying as we got to the top of the mountain. It didn't matter because I knew I could always say the wind made my eyes water and anyways Mairead was ahead of me so she didn't see. When I saw her at the top with the sun behind her, she looked so cool and strong that for a brief minute I thought maybe I would tell her about school and cutting myself and doing Rachel's home-work. It was only for a minute though and soon I forgot about that – no good having Mairead think I was a loser.

We walked for miles down the other side of the moun-tain to the shore and she showed me her secret place which was a sort of cave that you could only get to at certain times of the tides. She said she went there when it got too crazy at home and I was so lucky not to have younger brothers and sisters to take care of and that she secretly wished she could be me. That sort of settled whether or not I'd be telling Mairead about the Rachel business – no use telling her what my life was really like.

That night when we were getting into our pyjamas Mairead noticed some of the scratches on my arm and asked me what they were from and I had to lie and say my best friend Rachel had an adorable kitten who loved climbing up my arms and I knew she believed me because (a) I was an expert liar at that point and (b) she never in a hundred years would have believed how those scratches really got there.

By the time I got into bed I had forgotten all about cutting myself and I didn't think of anything else but being in the most beautiful place in the world with the sea putting me to sleep. It was a fierce winter sea but I loved it and was never afraid of the sound of storms.

*

It was the best Christmas ever. Sean and Darren nearly killed each other trying to be the first to get downstairs to see what Santa left which of course woke everybody even though it was about six in the morning. We all went into the living room and the tree was lit and it was still dark and the wind sounded like it was going to blow the house down but not really. There were loads of presents under the tree and pandemonium as the twins got confused about whose were whose and they opened a nail polish set that was meant for me.

I felt so happy I thought I would cry again – that happens a lot these days – especially when Uncle Brian lit the fire and Aunt Sinead made hot chocolate which both the twins immediately spilled and no one seemed to mind.

I got some really nice presents including a gorgeous jumper from Top Shop that I really wanted but never thought I'd get and lots of books and some pens with very narrow nibs in lots of excellent colours. So I really – and I mean really – had no idea that I would get anything else. Everyone started whispering to each other and I didn't know what was going on and Dad said, 'Back in a minute.'

Then Mairead said, 'Will you help me get the eggs, Marie?'

I love collecting the eggs from their crazy chickens that live at the side of the house. And even though it was really windy and wild outside we just put on some wellies over our pyjamas and grabbed two of the long raincoats they have hanging by the door and went out back. When we got there Dad came around the side of the house with *the* most beautiful cocker spaniel and said, 'Marie do you mind taking this monster off my hands? It's yours after all!'

Turns out Dad had caved in and finally got a dog. I had given up asking ages ago because I thought he'd never change his mind.

The dog was a shared present for me and Mam. I think Dad thought that would be a good way to get her to exercise. Mam came out then too and we all just hugged each other. Dad said I could name him so I called him Pause which Dad thought was very funny – no one would know it wasn't 'Paws' because you don't get much opportunity to write down a dog's name. Everyone loved it and he does have four white paws so any way you look at it, it was a perfect name.

On Steven's Day Mam and I were up first so we took Pause for a walk. Mam didn't walk that fast which was a drag for Pause who had to keep running back to us but it was very good for chatting. She asked me if I wanted to talk about school or anything – she said I'd gone very quiet at home these past few months. Every part of me wanted to tell her everything but I knew once I started it would all come out and then the holiday would be wrecked so I kind of did a fake laugh and said, 'I'm grand' and then I ran to get Pause. When I got back to her she looked a bit sad but didn't bring it up again and we laughed about the chaos at the house and everything seemed okay again.

In fact everything was going perfectly until New Year's Eve. At seven, Mrs MacDonagh from next door came over and plopped herself in front of the TV. Even though she was technically in charge it was really up to me and Mairead to watch the younger kids which basically meant making sure that Gemma didn't wake up and that the twins didn't fight over the video games they got and didn't overdo it with treats as sugar made them even more hyper.

The adults were going to the Red Fox to ring in the New Year. Dad said what he says every New Year's Eve, 'Well I guess I won't see you till next year,' which made the twins burst into tears.

Anyway after they left I don't know why but I turned on my phone. Mainly to see if Stella had texted me back – I had sent her a text at Christmas but I think she was away because I didn't hear from her and she also doesn't use her phone much. I was so busy with Pause and Brunt that I didn't even think of checking before then.

And there they were: six new messages. I felt sick and at first I wasn't going to look at them. But I knew I'd be distracted thinking about them so finally I opened them and all the goodness of Connemara couldn't save me. It had just been a distraction. Next week I would be back to the real world.

Are you coming to the party at Rachel's?

You could wear that lovely red outfit from Halloween

Want to meet before at Jill's?

Have you done all the English homework?

Hope you got a hair straightener for Xmas – you need one

And this one, which was the worst:

Don't worry your secret is safe with us

Now I don't know who they were from but the fact there were six gave me a fair clue.

I'm not sure why the secret one got to me. I felt like I had so many secrets now – from Mam and Dad and the teachers and Mairead – that I didn't even know what the text meant, just that it made me feel sick.

I volunteered to read to the boys while Mairead heated up Gemma's milk. Mairead couldn't believe she was off the hook and said I was the best. If only she knew.

Best liar.

Best fool.

Best keep quiet.

*

I was nervous all the way home from Connemara. Pause was amazing. He slept almost the whole time at my feet. We stopped to eat halfway and Mam could not believe

I wasn't having anything. When Dad went to the loo I almost told her. I almost said, 'I don't want to do Rachel's homework any more. I know it must be all my fault but I don't want to go to school. I want to stay in Connemara.' But instead I just said I had cramps so she wouldn't say anything else.

When we got home I still had two days before school started back. That night I heard Other Marie again. My cheeks were wet with tears when I woke and I genuinely don't know how they got there.

The next afternoon I asked Mam to tell me more about our Other Marie and she looked surprised but then she hugged me and we sat on the couch and snuggled under the felt blanket with horses on it.

She said that it was a cot death. It was nobody's fault although she felt for a long time that she must have done something wrong. She said that people were very nice and kind but when she became pregnant again they acted like she should just forget about the first Marie – but she never did. And, although I will never really get why they called us the same name, I do get the part about not forgetting. She said she was glad I had asked about her and that it was healthy to talk about difficult things and never good to hold things in.

Then we were both quiet for a long time and I almost told her about everything but I wanted the quiet to go on and I wanted her to think I was grown up and I certainly didn't want to give her anything new to worry about so I said nothing. It got dark without us noticing and then Dad came in and turned on the light and got a fright because he hadn't seen us sitting there and then we ordered pizza.

That night I started to read the book Mairead gave me for Christmas. And it was fantastic. It was about a girl who gets kidnapped at an airport and taken to the outback in Australia and just when you think she's going to be stuck there for ever she gets bitten by a snake and the kidnapper takes her to the hospital even though he knows he'll get caught. Now that's the kind of book I want to write some day – full of unexpected moral dilemmas and brave heroines.

11

I wasn't expecting the first week back to go smoothly so it didn't surprise me when Rachel came up to me at my locker and said in that fake voice she seems to use just for me, 'Happy New Year Marie. Hope you got our texts? Ready for our Friday homework?'

Claire and Jade were standing beside her smirking and I knew it was Rachel's not so subtle way of letting me know it might be a new year but some things were not going to change. So I just kept looking in my locker and said yeah and then they moved on.

After that I really did not expect any of the Stupid Six to talk to me so you can imagine my amazement when Jill was actually nice to me in Home Ec. I don't think one of the Stupid Six has ever had a real conversation with me. I thought things would have changed once they saw that I kept my mouth closed about the homework.

Mind you it wasn't really a conversation as Jill did all the talking and I just kept nodding my head. We were put together as partners for making scones and she started talking about her brother and how he ran away from home over Christmas. He's two years older than her and he came in really late from a party and his parents found out he had been drinking and then they said he was grounded and then he said, 'I've had it I'm out of here,' and then that's when Ms Coveney came over and said, 'Make sure all the chat is scone chat only girls.' And although she wasn't really mad she said it in a loud voice so of course everyone heard.

After class in the hall I heard Rachel giving out to Jill for talking so much to me. 'And for God's sake don't tell her any of our business. She isn't one of us you know.'

Jill said, 'Oh come on, she isn't that bad.'

And Rachel said, 'Are you serious? God you are so soft Jill – you'd talk to anyone. Okay, if you think she's so great why don't we give her the ABC test?'

I didn't know what they meant by the ABC test but I did feel kind of happy about how Jill had talked about me. Maybe the other five are okay when they can get away from Rachel's spell.

It wasn't long before I found out what the ABC test was. We were in the bathroom – me and Rachel and Jill and Claire.

Gail, who is very quiet and very very tall, came in to wash some ink off her hands. I don't really know her well but she sometimes talks to me at my locker and she seems nice enough. Rachel said really loudly, 'Who wants gum? Its sugar free.' Then she proceeded to give some to

Claire and Jill and made a big deal of giving me some and then she said, 'Oh sorry Gail do you want some too? Marie, will you pass her this.' And then Rachel took a piece of wet chewed gum out of her mouth and handed it over for me to take – and suddenly I got that ABC stood for Already Been Chewed. I could feel my neck and face get hot and I froze, not sure what to do.

Eventually Gail left and Rachel put the gum back in her mouth and they all laughed their heads off and when they finally calmed down Rachel said, 'Okay Marie you didn't exactly pass the test but who knows one of these days you might get to have lunch with us anyway.'

Then they left and I just washed my hands for about ten minutes and I wished I had something with me to cut myself. I had to settle for scratching the scab off the cut on the back of my ankle. But it didn't really make a difference. There's nothing like a fresh cut to really take your mind off things.

I made a secret New Year's resolution to stop cutting

myself because I know it isn't a normal thing to do but sometimes when I haven't had a great day I find it impossible not to think about it.

Mam made a New Year resolution to walk every day and she didn't seem to have any trouble sticking to it. She took Pause out twice a day and it really was starting to pay off. She already looked a bit better. Dad told me that she was going to Weight Watchers' meetings on Tuesday nights and the meetings were held at my school. He said, 'Don't tell her I told you. She's a bit sensitive about it.'

*

I read somewhere that it takes twenty-one days to break a habit so if I start tomorrow and don't cut for twenty-one days then maybe by then things will be better at school and I won't want to cut any more.

Last night I heard Other Marie crying again. She didn't wake me once when we were in Connemara.

When will it stop?

*

February seemed to go on for ages. It was rainy and wet every day for weeks and my twenty-one days were up long ago and I still hadn't broken any habits.

Mam kept asking why I hadn't read the Christmas books she gave me. I thought she should relax. They were only books and I just didn't have the time. I didn't know what was so hard to understand about that. She was starting to really get on my nerves.

And even though she was being the annoying one I was the one who was getting in trouble. Dad was always saying, 'Don't snap at your mother Marie.' And so I didn't snap. I didn't say anything. Stella was the only one who seemed normal which shows you how normal my universe was at that time.

Finally something interesting happened. The Principal made an announcement over the intercom about two contests that were coming up. One was an art project where you had to design a poster for the National Guide Dogs of Ireland Association. The winner would have their poster used in a campaign to highlight awareness of the National Guide Dogs of Ireland. I can't really draw so I wouldn't be entering that.

The other contest was for Creative Writing – you had to write a short story and it could be about absolutely anything you wanted. The three best ones were going to go on the school website and be published in the year-book as well. I would really love to be a published author.

*

I didn't think Rachel meant it when she said I might have lunch with them one day but I still sort of looked over at their table whenever I came into the lunchroom. Most days I sat with Stella and I really wanted to ask her if she was going to enter the poster competition seeing as she was the best artist in the class. And it would be good practice for when she entered the workforce and was a professional artist. She said she wasn't sure about the contest and by the way she was going to be either a scientist or a detective.

Then I told her about my pipe dream – which is an expression I like even though I don't really like anything to do with smoking – which was to be a published writer. Stella didn't act like that was unrealistic or anything. She asked me if I'd written anything yet and I told her I write in my diary and sometimes I write in my files. I said the files are based on real people but I might use them for characters in a story and if she liked I'd let her look at them. She just said okay and kept eating her lunch.

I tried again to convince her to enter the poster contest and said she could use Pause as a model if she wanted. I knew that might get her because she absolutely loves Pause. She came with us to Sandymount Strand to have a run on the beach last Sunday. Well Pause ran. Stella and I kind of walked fast and kept throwing him the green tennis ball that he loves and Dad sat in the car and read the paper. Stella's not allowed to get a pet of any kind because her brother has asthma and is allergic to all animal hair. Stella said, 'Pause would make a great poster dog.'

Then out of the blue just after Stella said that, Rachel started waving her hands in the air signalling for me to come over. At first I didn't even think she meant me. When I realised she did I felt kind of bad just leaving Stella but she didn't even look at me when I got up. She just kept folding up her wrapper from her sandwich into a really small square so I figured she didn't really mind.

Later when I thought about the whole idea of Pause posing I realised Pause doesn't really look like a guide dog – I think they use golden retrievers or Labradors or German shepherds, and Pause is just a small cocker spaniel. I have a feeling Stella might already know that and she was probably just being nice.

When I got to the table I sat beside Jade. They made room for me but I didn't really know what they were talking about. It was as if they talked in their own private code. I was glad to be there but kind of looking forward to going back to class when Rachel leaned over and said, 'So Marie, do you want to come to my place after school on Friday? We're going to wax Claire's legs. You can walk with us – I usually get a drive but my mom can't pick me up on Fridays.' I just said okay and hoped I wasn't blushing and I felt pretty good the rest of the day.

12

When I got home I decided to start on my story. It was hard to get going. I don't really have the energy for anything except cutting.

What if everyone is going to wax their legs at Rachel's? I don't even have any hair on my legs and they'll see all the cut marks I have and then they'll never ask me to hang out with them again. I thought that the tops of my legs would be a good spot to cut because I intend to stop soon and hopefully the marks will be healed by the time I have to wear shorts.

I've been thinking a lot about Anne Frank these days. I don't mean to romanticise and say she was so lucky to live in an attic in hiding and then be caught but she is the most famous teenage writer ever and I think the most amazing thing about her diary is she didn't write about how horrible the Nazis were, she kind of just talked about her life. So I guess against all the odds she was an optimist. I used to be one too. But I don't feel too optimistic these days. Everything just seems hard.

*

I shouldn't have wasted any time worrying about going to Rachel's because it almost all went really well. I couldn't believe that Rachel got a drive home most days – her house is really close. Down the side of the school until the road comes out near Eddie Rocket's. Run across Rathmines Road – the traffic is mental there, you have to run even when the light is green for crossing – and then up the side street towards the park. On three sides of the park are huge Georgian houses and of course Rachel lives in one of them. It's just her and her mam and dad and her sister in that mansion! Rachel's bedroom is the size of our living room. She has a bay window overlooking the park and a bathroom that is just for her and her sister.

Claire started setting up a towel on the desk so we could do our nails. Rachel said something about how her sister was out of leg wax so we were all going to do our nails instead and then she produced about ten different bottles of nail polish that she took from her sister's room which made me think she must be an amazing sister to let her use them. But then Rachel said, 'She'll never even notice – she has loads. She's probably out buying more right now.' Then she came and sat beside me and said, 'We've been thinking, since we already have a Marie maybe we should give you a real nickname. We thought Maimie might be nice. What do you think?'

Maimie.

Not Other Marie.

I thought it sounded gorgeous and the idea of having a name all to myself – not a dead baby's name – made me feel really good. I tried not to be too enthusiastic and just said, 'Okay that's fine.' The rest of the time I didn't really say much but I felt okay and everyone laughed when I chose the really light pink nail polish because it's called 'Nude'.

Claire asked Rachel if her dad was still taking her to Disneyland Paris on the March break. Rachel sort of snapped back at her, 'Why wouldn't he?' and gave her that look that really shuts people up. I felt sort of bad for Claire because it seemed like she was just making conversation.

Rachel walked me to the front door and when I got there she said, 'Oh, one last thing Maimie. To be part of our group you have to give us some interesting fact about someone that we don't already know. We were thinking maybe you could find out something about Stella – the weird girl who's always repeating herself. You hang out with her sometimes don't you?'

I said I didn't really know anything about her but Rachel wouldn't give up. 'I'm sure you'll think of something Maimie. See you Monday.'

And just like that everything felt wrong. Why did Rachel have to ruin everything by asking me to get something on Stella?

I went home and took off my nail polish and didn't even tell Mam and Dad my new nickname. I guess that would have to wait for when I knew it really was mine.

*

On Monday I noticed that Stella was having lunch with Gail and I wondered if she would tell Stella about the gum incident. I really hoped not. I could imagine Stella's disappointment if she thought I was that kind of person. I was just headed over to their table when Rachel waved at me to come over to them. I don't know why I didn't just say then and there, 'No thanks, you aren't really my type.' I guess part of me was happy to think maybe I was their type so I went over and right away Rachel asked, 'So any news on you know who?'

I was already sitting at this point and it would have been awkward getting up if I had nothing to say so I just blurted out, 'She's allergic to peanuts and even a small bit makes her face turn blue and she has to go to the hospital.' I felt sick as the words came out of my mouth. It was as if someone else was saying them. I remembered how I swore not to tell anyone and now I was afraid Rachel would tell everyone. Rachel looked quite pleased at this bit of information and she said, 'Well done Maimie. You're one of us now.'

The next day at lunch I was sitting with the six again when Stella walked by and Rachel said to her, 'Hey Stella, want one of my Plenty bars? I have two.'

Everyone knows that the plenty in Plenty bars means

plenty of peanuts. Stella just looked at Rachel and then she looked at me and said, 'No thanks. I don't feel like dying today.' Then she walked away and everyone laughed like crazy. I knew Stella could hear them laughing and I knew Stella would know I had told them about her. I wanted to run after her and say sorry but I knew it was too late so I just got up and said I was going to the toilet.

*

When I woke up the next day the very first thing I thought of was the way Stella looked when Rachel asked her about the Plenty bar and I really didn't want to go to school. But I knew my mam would just take me to the doctor if I said I didn't feel well. She's kind of extreme that way. You can't just have a headache or a cold – she always thinks it's going to turn into something life-threatening and she says, 'Let's get things checked out to be sure.'

When I got to my locker, Jill and Claire and Rachel

were all waiting for me. I didn't have anything to say and I was just closing my locker when Stella came up to me and said, 'It's okay if you don't want to be my friend be my friend. Here are your files back.'

Rachel has a radar for anything to do with her so she was suddenly interested and said, 'Files! Oh let's see them Maimie.' I took them from Stella and put them in my bag and as she walked away I heard Stella saying, 'Maimie? Maimie?' I told Rachel I'd show her later and we went to class.

Luckily every one of the six has the memory of a goldfish so the files weren't mentioned again that day. I wonder if Stella said it in front of them to get back at me for telling her secret?

At the end of the day Rachel said, 'Don't forget tomorrow. Eddie Rocket's. Be there or be square.'

Every bit of me wanted to say, 'Well guess what Rachel. I have other plans and you can't tell me what to do.' But I didn't say anything except, 'Okay.'

That night I tried to work on my story but I couldn't think of anything to write. So I tried reading because Mam is right – I've hardly read anything in ages. And even though I'm just rereading (for the third time) Jacqueline Wilson's book *My Secret Diary* I couldn't concentrate even though it is a very good book. It's all about Jacqueline Wilson's actual childhood and how she always wanted to be a writer and she also loved Anne Frank. I put it down on page six and it took me ages to fall asleep and wouldn't you know it I heard Other Marie crying again.

I haven't heard her in ages and I thought it was a thing of the past. I could hardly drag myself out of bed the next day and Mam said, 'Maybe we should get you checked out.' I didn't have the heart to tell her that I knew exactly what was wrong with me and that no doctor would have a cure for being a terrible friend and hearing things in the night so I just said maybe and then I went to school.

13

I really didn't want to go to Eddie Rocket's after school. I wished I was on a team or in the band so I could have a good excuse. The basketball practices and games were always on a Wednesday afternoon. So was the band practice. But I could hardly start one of them suddenly at this point in the year. I should have listened to Dad when he was encouraging me to sign up for something in September.

I convinced myself Eddie Rocket's would be fine and

now that I was in with them it would be an opportunity to tell them I thought the gum thing with Gail was a bit mean. So I decided I would go but I also decided to talk to Gail before going and tell her I was sorry about the gum thing and not to worry about the stupendously Stupid Six.

I tried to get my books out of my locker as fast as I could so I could find Gail and still have time to walk with the others to Eddie Rocket's. If I had been a bit more observant I would have realised that Gail hadn't been in all day.

While I was still at my locker Stella came up and asked me where I was going in such a hurry. She said it in such a nice way that I could tell she wasn't mad at me, that she just wanted things to be normal but I knew she belonged to a different part of my life and I didn't want her to come to Eddie Rocket's so I just said, 'Never mind,' and ran off.

I was the last one to arrive at Eddie Rocket's and since Rachel made up a rule that the last one has to pay for her, I ordered a chocolate Oreo shake for her and an ice water for me. I pretended that was what I really wanted but the reality was that after paying for Rachel's I didn't have any more money.

We got a booth at the back and Rachel looked kind of excited. She said, 'Okay so you know how Miss Featherston is the yearbook coordinator? Well she asked me to do a report for the yearbook. It has to be about the chocolate bar sale to raise money for the new gym. She said she asked me because Mr McGuire told her my English assignments have really improved. Thank you for that Maimie. You don't mind doing the article too do you?'

Well yes I did mind. I wanted to be a published author. I wanted to start with my story in the yearbook and then progress to magazine articles and blogs and when I accepted the Nobel Prize for Literature I wanted to say it had all started with my school yearbook and that would be an inspiration to young writers everywhere so yes I did mind.

But she didn't even wait to see what I thought. She just said, 'And I have a really good idea for it.' She passed me a yellow disposable camera and I felt a bit sick. Maybe just because it reminded me of the camera they find in the shark's stomach at the end of the film *Open Water* and you just know the shark ate the two idiots who got separated from their group when they were deep sea diving and then got abandoned in the middle of the ocean. It's a very good movie and based on a true story and I'm sorry if this ruins the end if you haven't seen it but to be honest anyone could tell from the beginning it wasn't going to end well.

Rachel went on to say she had found out something very interesting about the school. Apparently Weight Watchers held meetings there on Tuesday from seven to eight. I could feel my neck and face getting hot when she said that. She kept going. 'So here's the plan: Jade and Claire – you meet some of them coming out and try to sell them some chocolate bars and then Maimie can take their pictures and we can use the pictures to go with the article. What do you think?'

Everyone sorted of laughed nervously and then Jill said, 'We can make the headline, "Fatties Help Keep Us Fit",' which Jade and Claire thought was the funniest thing they had ever heard.

They had just started to calm down when Rachel looked at me and said, 'I think you know exactly who you can take a picture of, don't you Marie?' (She said Marie – not Maimie – which sounded kind of ominous.) I looked at her and of course I knew who she meant.

Mam.

Mam who I loved with all my heart even if I didn't always show it.

Suddenly I felt like I couldn't breathe and I needed to get out of there, to get as far away as possible from the Secret Six. My heart was really beating hard and tears were suddenly streaming down my face. Tears for all the times I was embarrassed to be seen with Mam. I needed to see her and tell her I'd never betray her like that.

I actually don't remember running out of the restaurant. I do remember grabbing my bag and knocking over the water and then needing to find Mam. I ran as fast as I could out of the restaurant and onto the street right in the path of an oncoming van.

Later the van driver swore blind that the sun was in his eyes and he just didn't see me run out. I felt a bit sorry for him because I was running very fast so I think he didn't have a chance.

Maybe I was running that fast because of the adrenalin in my body. Apparently adrenalin can do amazing things. I read about a mother who lifted up a car with her bare hands because her son was trapped underneath. Also I read about a woman in Australia who grabbed her baby right out of the mouth of a mad dingo that was trying to run away with it. And a man in Florida who actually knocked a shark unconscious by hitting it between the eyes while the shark, which had already taken a chunk out of his leg, was coming back for more. I'm not sure I believe that one but I do think adrenalin has a lot to answer for.

Stella told me later that while they were waiting for the ambulance the girls were crying at the door and no one noticed her across the street so she picked up my bag and took it home which is a good thing because my files were in it. But believe me, at the time, the files were the last thing on my mind.

14

I was in a coma for nine days although when I woke up I couldn't tell you how long it had been. Time is very different when you're unconscious and strange things can happen when your body is halfway between being alive and not.

I once read about a girl from Russia who had an accident and after she woke up from her coma she started speaking fluent German even though she'd never spoken a word in her life before. Also there is a man in Mexico who never drank a day in his life and after forty-five days in a coma he sat up straight in the bed and shouted for the nurses to get him a whiskey and then he fell back into his coma and woke up two days later and didn't remember a thing. But for me it's not what happened after the coma but during it that is the really interesting part.

First of all, yes it's true: when you're in a coma you can hear people talking (although they sound like they're under water). So remember if you are in a room with someone in a coma don't start saying personal things like how awful they look because it's very possible they will hear you and when you're in a coma you already feel pretty bad.

I could make out Mam crying and Dad talking and a nurse with a loud Cork accent and a doctor with a very low voice and later on Stella's voice was there too. But mostly what I remember were the dreams.

Some of them were very scary and I kept having the same one over and over that I was being put in the basement of the hospital at night all by myself and there was no way to get back to the normal part of the hospital. One night I started crying except even though the sound was coming from my mouth it wasn't really me – it was Other Marie making the sound.

Another time I was in a room that was all white and I could hear Other Marie crying again so I walked through one of the walls and came into a room on the other side of it. I was in a bedroom but when I looked down I couldn't see my body. I could still hear the crying. It was coming from a cot in the corner, a yellow cot with white sides, and in it was a baby. Other Marie.

I looked around the room and everything was exactly as Mam had described it – the wallpaper with yellow and white stripes, the rocking chair which is at Aunt Kate's house now and the little white dresser with a box on it. A beautiful wooden box. The same box that I found in Mam's dresser. The box with the letters.

I wanted to go and touch Marie and tell her I was her

sister and she didn't need to cry any more but before I could I felt a tugging at my arms and the nurse with the Cork accent was fixing a tube in my hand.

I wanted so badly to get back to the room but I didn't know how and so for ages I just heard the voices and slept and didn't dream at all. I heard Mam crying again and I wanted to tell her I was all right but soon I was asleep and in the room again.

Mam was in the room too and still crying but quietly and sitting in the rocking chair and holding a little blue and white dress with a tiny pocket. Marie's dress. Marie wasn't there.

Then Mam went to the box and took out a shell, and I knew it was the shell she told me about, the one she found on the beach before Marie was born. Mam was right – it did look like a butterfly. I watched as she wrapped it in some yellow tissue paper and put it in the pocket of the dress, put the dress carefully on top of the dresser and went to the window to close the yellow curtains. Then I saw my dad at the door to the room. Just standing there looking at Mam. 'I'm ready,' she said. 'You carry the dress and I'll follow you downstairs in a minute.'

Dad went to get the dress but before he picked it up he looked over at my mam and went to give her a hug.

I don't know why I did what I did next. I think I wanted to make things better and maybe if Mam still had the shell she wouldn't feel so sad. I knew Mam and Dad couldn't see me so I went over to the dress and took the tissue paper with the shell out of the pocket and carefully put it in the box that was on the dresser. When I turned to look at my parents they were gone and I was in the hospital bed and the voices didn't sound under water any more and I opened my eyes.

I got a bit of a fright because the first thing I saw was very black hair and then I heard the voice that went with it and even though she kind of looked like a fortune-teller her hair was so black, when she talked it was the Cork accent I had heard before when I was kind of under water and I knew I was back.

15

After I woke up, when everyone – the doctors, Mam
and Dad, the Gardaí – asked me what happened, I said
I didn't remember. I never wanted Mam to know what
Rachel's plan had been. I said I didn't remember why I
was running and everyone just left it at that.

Or I thought they left it at that.

The day I went home from the hospital Mam came to
help me pack and then Dr Heaney came in. He always
called me 'young lady' but other than that he was quite

nice. He stood at the end of the bed and said I was a very fortunate young lady, the cracked ribs would heal with time and the bruises all along the left side of my leg and all the way up my side would go away soon too. And as for my escaping any head injuries or broken bones, he just shook his head and said, 'You must have been born under a very lucky star. Take it easy young lady.' Then he gave my mam a prescription for painkillers and told her I was not to go back to school for five more weeks, which meant it would be May by the time I went back.

After he left, another doctor came in who didn't really look like a doctor – more like a teacher. Mam said she was Dr Flynn and she wanted to talk to me and that Mam would stay if I liked or we could talk privately. I thought that was pretty weird so I said Mam could stay. Dr Flynn said they couldn't help noticing some marks on my arms and legs and did I want to talk about how they got there. I said I didn't thank you very much and kept on packing.

What I didn't realise until I felt Mam's arms around me was that I was crying when I said that and then I couldn't stop. I didn't want to give away Rachel's plan and I almost told her about doing Rachel's homework and seeing Marie but all I said was, 'I was just experimenting and I won't do it any more.'

I know that wasn't the complete truth but I certainly didn't want to spend too much time thinking about it. Stella says it's hard to really say what's in your head and it's almost impossible for people to hear what you're really saying so most of the time they fill in the blanks with their own imaginations. So I left lots of room for their imaginations and soon I stopped crying and I finished packing and went home.

And even though I hadn't said out loud what had happened, somehow the crying felt as good as the cutting and I had a feeling it wouldn't be so hard to break the habit now.

When I got home I watched lots of TV and did some

baking and loads of sleeping – which the doctor said would be the norm for a while. It was a bit boring but my ribs were too sore to walk much so I didn't go anywhere except to see Dr Flynn once a week.

Mam said it was just until I went back to school and the appointment was at Dr Flynn's office which was just the first floor of a regular house so I didn't really mind going. Mam said it would be a time when I could talk about anything I wanted but most days I just sat there saying nothing and neither did Dr Flynn so she has a pretty easy job if you ask me.

Once she asked, 'Is there anything you feel like saying to Rachel?'

Okay, I hadn't been completely silent. I had talked a bit about Rachel and the Stupid Six.

Inside I was dying to say yes I know exactly what I'd like to say. I'd like to say, 'You are a total bitch. What gives you the right to be so awful to people?' Of course I didn't say that out loud. I just looked out the window and I saw that there were flowers in the yard and I hadn't even noticed it was spring.

During those weeks Stella came and visited me and told me about things that had happened at school. She said not to feel bad that I was in a coma for St Patrick's Day and the midterm break. She said nobody did anything interesting. Even Rachel who had been bragging for weeks that she was 'going to Europe with her dad' ended up not going for some reason.

She also said the Stupid Six spent a lot of the time I was in the hospital walking around school with tears in their eyes. The teachers all thought they were so sensitive – traumatised by worry about their friend.

Stella saw right through that. She overheard them in the loo talking. 'What if Marie tells them it's our fault she ran into the road. What if she tells about the plan. Can we get blamed for the accident?' This is my favourite part: Rachel actually said, 'I am way too young to get charged with manslaughter. It will ruin my chances for anything after school.' Someone should have told that girl that (a) I wasn't dead so the manslaughter bit didn't make any sense and (b) her chances were already pretty limited.

Mam told me that Stella had gone to the hospital to visit me every day at the exact same time. She arrived at 4.45 and left at 5.35 and always had a book with her and she read and talked to me non-stop. Also she walked Pause every day. Mam and Dad were so busy coming to see me at the hospital that Stella was worried he wasn't getting enough walking so every day after school she took him to the park before she came to see me. It felt like we had become friends again without trying, that somehow our lives were sort of mixed up together.

I knew I had to talk to her about breaking my promise but when I brought it up Stella just said, 'It's okay. Let's forget about it. And anyways I got back at Rachel and her idiots.' Then she told me she gave them my files and I nearly had a heart attack. 'It's okay,' said Stella. 'Let's just say I doctored them all. They looked exactly like yours with their names on them and everything but I rewrote them completely in fake Irish. There are just enough real words to drive them crazy and the rest is complete nonsense. They spend every lunch hour poring over Irish dictionaries. The teachers can't figure out what's gotten into them.'

Then she handed me my real files, and I nearly burst into tears I was so relieved and so impressed by her revenge on my behalf. I gave her a hug and said thanks even though I didn't want to keep files any more. And certainly not files on that lot. What a waste of time.

Stella helped me shred them in my dad's paper shredder and then we took Pause to the park.

I was so glad Stella and I were friends again because ever since I got out of the hospital I had been dying to tell her about my vision or whatever it was. I knew I had to start at the beginning and explain about Other Marie crying so the last part would make sense. And I knew she wouldn't make fun or roll her eyes or say, 'But you were in a coma – it was probably just a dream.'

And I knew she would help me figure out how it was possible that I had time-travelled. Because that's what happened. I had seen my mam and dad and my sister in another time. And I had changed things. I moved the butterfly shell. I know I did.

My birthday was the Friday before I went back to school. Dad had to leave early for work before I got up so he left my card on the mantelpiece and said there would be presents after dinner. The card was from my mam and dad and was covered with sunflowers and inside was a book voucher for twenty euro. And behind the card was a tiny gold box with two chocolates from Leonidas.

Stella was coming over for a sleepover after dinner so Mam, Dad and I had a family party first. We ordered Chinese food, and it was delicious. I had sweet and sour chicken and spring rolls, Dad had Kung Po duck and Mam believe it or not didn't order anything and made a salad with tuna instead – though she did have a few of the prawn crackers with it. She's on a health kick and even her only daughter's thirteenth birthday doesn't seem to be reason enough to get off it. I think she's kind of amazing because I could not imagine being in the same room as sweet and sour chicken and not wanting to eat it.

For dessert we had my favourite cake: marble cake with chocolate icing and yes candles and yes they sang 'Happy Birthday' and sort of harmonised at the end when they sang it and Pause sort of joined in though I think he was just whining because Dad had put a stupid party hat on him. Pause was trying so hard to get at the cake that I blew out the candles really fast and forgot to make a wish.

After dinner I got more presents. The first one was from Dad. He had taken a picture of me with Pause on Sandymount Strand and he got it framed and I love it. It looks like it should have a caption with it because Pause is caught in mid-air with the Frisbee in his mouth and I'm sort of clapping behind him and wearing my favourite red hoodie.

The next present was really a surprise. It was a denim jacket just like the one I had pointed out to Mam in the Warehouse but this one was from Urban Outfitters. I couldn't believe it. It's a gorgeous shop and I've never had anything from there before. I tried it on and it was perfect. Also I got an iTunes voucher and some Turkish delight which I think is even better than chocolate though I know that's hard to believe. Then they gave me the best one of all that they had saved for last: a book with a beautiful soft leather cover the colour of sand. And when I opened it I saw that it was a diary. The part you write on comes out so you can replace the inside once it's full so the leather cover can be my cover forever. I can't wait to start using it. I used to think a diary had to start on the first of January and be for each year but I think I might change that tradition and start a new one each birthday.

I went to lie down for a rest before Stella came. A few

minutes later, Mam came into my room and said, 'I have another present for you Marie – it isn't wrapped and I need to explain it to you.' Then from behind her back she brought out the box. *The* box. The beautiful wooden one from my dream, the one with the letters. The Marie box.

She held it on her lap and said, 'This is full of letters you might like to read and at the bottom is something very special that I thought was gone but isn't. You'll think I'm a bit crazy but I'll fill you in when you come to it.'

I kind of held my breath because I had a feeling I knew what it would be. I took the box and said thanks and opened it and there was the pile of letters – letters I had already seen though I couldn't say that to Mam. I opened the first one.

Dear Marie who would be one today,
I wish you were here – to start to walk
– to call me Mama – to smile and already
have favourite things.
I love you.

I wasn't sure I wanted my birthday to be all about this much missed Other Marie but Mam kept smiling at me so I kept going.

The next one was also to Marie:

To Marie who would be two today,

Dear Marie

I have a secret. You are the first to know. I haven't even told your father yet.

I'm having another baby. In eight months he or she will be here. If it's a boy we'll call him Paul Joseph – after your two grandfathers. And if it's a girl we'll call her Marie. You are Marie Hannah. Marie because I like it and Hannah after my mother. She will be Marie after you. And her second name will be Hope. After no one. Just because it is strong and because I hope she will be too.

Of course I have to talk about the names with your father but I have a feeling he'll agree.

I love you.

I opened the next letter and I couldn't believe it – it wasn't addressed to Other Marie. It was addressed to me. In fact, all the rest were to me. It wasn't a box of Other Marie after all. It was a box of me – of pictures and special things that had happened to me during each year. Mam had written them on my birthdays. So all the time I thought she was wishing the Other Marie was here, she was busy writing to me.

I almost started to cry I was so relieved.

Then Mam said, 'There's something else – under the letters.' I took the letters out and at the bottom of the box was a small square of yellow tissue paper. Paper I had seen before and touched before and had put in that very box. I just stared at it, and Mam began to talk. She said sometimes things happen that are just meant to be. 'I don't know why Marie had to leave this world so early but maybe that was meant to be. Do you remember when I told you I had found a special shell on the beach in Connemara and I thought it would bring good luck? And do you remember I said I buried it with her, that I put it in the pocket of her dress so it could be near her heart forever? Well I thought I did. And I can't explain how it got in the box or why I never saw it until last week. Every year I open this box to put in your letter and never before did I see it. Then on the morning of the day you woke up from your coma, I wrote part of your birthday letter before going to see you at the hospital. When I went to the box to put it at the bottom – so you would read them in order – there it was. The yellow tissue paper. And I knew at once it was my butterfly shell. I still don't know how it got there Marie. I guess that grief can do strange things to your memory. Or maybe it was just meant to be that you have it. I had the jeweller in the craft shop in the

Liberty Market put a small hole and a chain on it in case you want to wear it.'

In case I wanted to wear it? Of course I wanted to wear it! Just try getting me to take it off.

It was perfect, and I put it on immediately and gave Mam the biggest, hardest hug until she laughed and said, 'Okay Marie I still need to breathe.'

I don't know if it's possible that I moved the shell or if it was all a dream but I think Mam might be right that some things are meant to be.

Then the doorbell went and when I opened the door the first thing Stella said was, 'Abalone. Cool.'

16

My first day back went pretty well. The Stupid Six kept their distance and hardly looked at me and everyone else in the school had the exact opposite reaction. They were all really nice and came over to say hi to me even if I hardly knew them. I felt like a celebrity – 'The Girl Who Survived a Coma'.

The teachers were all very friendly and told me to take my time, and in Geography Miss Gilligan told me not to worry about the test they were having. It was on different kinds of rocks and where they are found. Miss Gilligan read out the questions. I didn't have anything else to do so I tried to answer them and even though it was on things they covered when I was off school, I didn't find it that hard. Miss Gilligan looked amazed I had even tried when I handed in my paper.

When I was at my locker getting my books to go home Rachel came up to me and just stood there for a minute. Then she looked me straight in the eye and said, 'I'm glad you're okay.'

And there it was. My big chance to say what I had rehearsed so many times in my head, to tell her what I really thought of her. But something stopped me and when I did speak all I said was, 'Okay, thanks,' and then she left.

I watched her as she walked away and something felt different. Not sure what exactly. Maybe she just didn't look so perfect any more.

I got through the first day without cutting myself – in fact I never even thought of it.

I was pretty tired when I got home but I worked on my story for the competition. I was nearly finished. It's about identical twins who are professional thieves and they provide alibis for each other because everyone thinks they are just one person. I read some of it to Stella to see what she thought. She said it was good but a bit far-fetched. Then she showed me her poster. It was fantastic. Most of the page was taken up with a big black circle that looked like the pupil of your eye and in the middle was a tiny yellow guide dog. That may sound weird but it completely grabbed your attention and made you think about how dark everything is if you are blind. I hope she wins.

The next day we got back our geography tests and I couldn't believe my mark. I don't think Miss Gilligan could believe it either because she kept asking me, 'Are you sure you didn't read this material while you were away?' I got 90 per cent, and Stella said, 'I knew it,' out loud in class.

On the way home she said, 'When I visited you at the hospital I used to tell you about what happened in school and for three days in a row I read you the lists of the different rocks and where they were from because I knew you probably didn't know anything about them. I wanted to prove that you could hear me even though you were in a coma. And then yesterday you knew everything on the test without even studying. So now I have proof!'

I'm not really sure about that except I guess in a way it proves she is my friend because she didn't give up on me in the hospital.

*

At the end of my first week back Mam told me at dinner that Aunt Sinead had just called and would I like to go on my own to Connemara in June for two weeks? I am old enough to take the train on my own and Uncle Brian will pick me up at the station in Galway.

I was so excited I jumped up to hug her when she

said, 'There is a small catch. They are minding a pregnant dog for their neighbours who are away and there's a
good chance she'll have the pups while you're there. And
the house is already crazy enough without adding Pause
to the mix so she'd rather you didn't bring him.' Even
though I love Pause to bits I knew Aunt Sinead was right.

But then I had a brainwave. I'd been trying to think
of some way to make it up to Stella for breaking my
promise and to thank her for minding Pause while I was
in the hospital. This was the perfect solution. She could
mind Pause for the two weeks. He loves her and she'd
probably walk him even more than I do. Her brother was
going to Irish College so her parents wouldn't object. I
couldn't wait to tell her.

*

The rest of May seemed to fly by and every day I felt
a bit stronger and not so sore. The Stupid Six still continued to keep well away from me which suited me fine

and on the last day of school I found out that my story, which I called 'Seeing Double', was on the shortlist, but we won't find out until September which one gets to be in the yearbook.

17

I left for Connemara two days after school ended. Mam and Dad and Pause all came to the train station to see me off. It was my first time travelling alone and I loved the feeling of being in charge. I sat by the window and by the time we were just a few miles out of Dublin I had fallen asleep. I think it was a combination of the sun beating down and me being so tired from everything.

I dreamed about meeting Fungie the Dolphin and in my dream I asked him if it really was him under the waves in my dad's pictures. I didn't get an answer because I woke up when the trolley came around. I bought some crisps and looked out the window the rest of the way.

Uncle Brian and Mairead picked me up at the station in Galway and then we drove to their house which took about a half hour. When I got there Aunt Sinead gave me a big hug and immediately noticed my butterfly shell. She asked me if she could see it so I took it off and she sat down in a kitchen chair just staring at it saying, 'Well I never.' Then she gave it back and told me it was the most beautiful piece of shell she had ever seen and tomorrow she would take me to the little strand where my mam had found it. She said it was a few miles away and we could take a lunch with us and hope the weather holds up.

*

It turned out the weather did hold up, and this has been the sunniest summer since 1995. Every evening after dinner I come to my favourite flat rock with my notebook and I write. The sea looks like it's dancing and when I look out to the light sparkling on it, everything about the past year is clear in my mind. Sometimes I miss Other Marie and I wonder if I'll ever hear her again. And although Stella never actually said she believes in ghosts, after I told her about Other Marie she said she thinks the only unusual thing is that spirits don't collide more often.

Stella can be very surprising sometimes.

Today at the exact same time as I was looking for a shell to bring back to her, I got a text. From Stella who hardly ever texts. Now *that's* synchronicity. It said

> boiling hot here. swam at the forty foot yesterday. held my breath for 1 min and 58 seconds. new personal best. Pause says hi

So now.

The cuts are nearly invisible and my tan really covers
them.
The accident seems like a long time ago.
and
The butterfly shell feels like it's been around my neck
forever.

And even though I'm not superstitious any more, sometimes when I touch it I have a really strong feeling that
next year is going to be a good one.

Acknowledgements

Thank you to my friends and early readers: Sheila White, Lorraine White, Gene Rooney, Jo Donohoe, Mary Kelly, Eleanor Methvan, Ann-Marie MacDonald, Baņuta Rubess, Stephanie Courtney and Aoife O Callaghan White. Thank you Jo Donohoe and John Devine for the peace of Kilmore Quay; and Rory Boyd and Ann Keating for the beauty of Achill. Thank you, Rosa Devine, for the photos, and Patrick Sutton for that very important introduction to Michael O'Brien.

To everyone at The O'Brien Press: Michael, thank you for taking a chance with me. And thank you, Helen Carr,

Kunak McGann and Emma Byrne, for your support and expertise. To my editor, Liz Hudson, a huge thank you for your patience, your rigorous reading and your sharp eye for detail. I hope we can do it again.

A very special thanks to Hilary Fannin and Michèle Forbes for your insight, friendship, coffee and endless encouragement. This book would certainly not have made it here without you.

And finally, Ed, Luke and Aoife, love and thanks always.